# THE
# DEATH
## IN THE
# WILLOWS

A RINEHART SUSPENSE NOVEL

A RINEHART SUSPENSE NOVEL

# THE
# DEATH
## IN THE
# WILLOWS

## Richard Forrest

HOLT, RINEHART AND WINSTON

*New York*

LIBRARY OF CONGRESS CATALOGING IN PUBLICATION DATA
Forrest, Richard, 1932–
The death in the willows.
(A Rinehart suspense novel)
I. Title.
PZ4.F72887Dc    [PS3556.0739]       813'.5'4      79–4116
ISBN 0-03-049296-3

First Edition

Designer: Trish Parcell
Printed in the United States of America
1 3 5 7 9 10 8 6 4 2

*In memory of the folks—*
*Georgia and Bill*

# THE
# DEATH
## IN THE
# WILLOWS

A RINEHART SUSPENSE NOVEL

1     The Wobblies didn't care for the Times Square area. In protective phalanx they flanked Lyon Wentworth as he walked
Forty-second Street toward the Port Authority Bus Terminal.
Two barbed tails switched in disapproval while long snouts pointed
disdainfully from adult book store to X-rated movie.

    Lyon blinked into the dying sun as he stopped at the corner of
Eighth Avenue to wait for the light to change. He felt the unseen
presence of his benign monster creations on either side and knew they
would glare at the passing menagerie with fire-red eyes as if screening
potential assassins from some archaic potentate.

    The Port Authority squats nearly in the geographical center of
Manhattan, its refurbished facade a hulking contrast to the immediate
surroundings. Looking south he could see the tip of the Minnesota
Strip where young Nordic girls, enticed from small farming communi-
ties, ambled in slow gait like neophyte sirens along nonexistent rocks
with eyes turned dull above smiles that fooled only the most blindly
lecherous. Further along Forty-second Street, young men bobbed
heads on high steps, another increment of this group that pretended
they were alive.

    As the light changed and the crowd propelled him across the street, the Wobblies began to fade, to reappear at another time and place. He felt the reassurance of the slender briefcase tucked under his arm that contained the contract from his publisher for his next children's book, *The Wobblies Find A Clue.*

It had been a good and satisfying day. The conference with his editor had gone well, his work had been appreciated, plans had been formulated, and he'd even received a passing smile from the editor in chief. The terminal entrance immediately expunged the glare of the sun and the macabre dance of the undead outside.

A scan of the departure board told him that he had time to spare before the bus to Middleburg, Connecticut. He walked to a small bar tucked in a corner of the terminal, slid onto a stool between two other men, and ordered a Dry Sack sherry.

"Sherry?" the bartender replied with a blink of rheumy eyes.

"Please."

"I got some muscatel that won't blind you."

"Harvey's Bristol Cream will do."

"A shot with a beer chaser's been popular today."

"Chivas Regal with a dash of soda."

"How about some all-purpose brandy that we can cut with something?"

Lyon nodded. Another loss in life's battles, but his good feelings were still strong enough to enable him to ignore it. He sipped the drink with a pretense it was something else and thought about Wobblies.

The three men sitting at the bar were of divergent natures and origins, brought to this place by coincidental destination with a departing bus; their only similarity was that two of them carried guns.

Willie Shep, the youngest, occupied the stool near the wall to Lyon's left. He wore Levi's, boots with high heels, and a multicolored shirt that fell loosely over his waist and successfully hid the flat .32 Walther PPK automatic tucked in the waistband of his trousers.

Willie sucked on a draft beer served in a large frosted glass. Within moments only a thin line of foam curled along his lip, and he stared angrily at the glass, as if fate had once again conspired to complicate his life. He jammed an impatient hand into his pocket, plunked a handful of change on the bar, and pushed three quarters, four nickels, and seven pennies toward the bartender.

2

The bartender looked at the assortment of change with a lethargy born of long wisdom in such matters and scooped it from the counter, ostentatiously leaving two pennies. He refilled Willie's glass, letting foam dribble down the side, and slid it across the bar. Willie wiped it with his index finger, and using the remaining pennies as eyes, drew a face, extended the finger in pistol fashion toward the center of the caricature, and made a *poo* sound from the corner of his mouth.

He gulped half the beer and glanced down at his wrist toward a watch no longer there. His eyes jerkily scanned the small room until they found a clock above the cash register and noted the time.

He had an intense, pointed face with a chin that jutted forward as if daring life to deal another blow. His medium build appeared slight due to a concave chest that he tried to hide by constantly hunching his shoulders forward. He seemed to writhe on the stool. His fingers played incessant nervous games, constantly becoming more agitated until he slid from the stool in an abrupt motion and took the few steps to the men's room.

The facility was empty and he threw the bolt on the door, urinated, zippered his pants, and slid the Walther from his waistband. Extracting the clip, he slammed it back in the gun and briefly considered activating the slide to pump a live round into the chamber. He decided otherwise; the gun's precarious position in his pants needed an extra safety factor. He replaced the gun and patted his rear pocket, which held two extra clips.

The door handle turned and he whirled, instinctively reaching for the gun. He dropped his hand back to his side, forced his body to relax, and nonchalantly slid back the door bolt and stepped out.

He stood next to the bar stool and let his fingers drum a tattoo on the bar. There were only minutes left—and then it would start.

The man on Lyon's right carried a .44 Smith and Wesson Magnum revolver in a long holster strapped to his left side and hidden from view by a light poplin jacket. He wore a heavy dark beard that covered half his face and a cap pulled low over his forehead, but his eyes were a sharp sky blue that impassively watched the bartender mix his martini. The bartending was contrary to his explicit directions, but he chose not to correct it as he turned his head slightly to observe Willie out of the corner of his eye.

The man's obvious nervousness ticked a warning bell. His eyes switched from Willie's pointed face down the sport shirt to the slight bulge at the waist. He knew what was under the shirt, and he rapidly considered the possibilities: undercover cop, hotgun, or denizen of the area carrying a piece for protection. The man's agitation ruled out cop, but increased the possibility that he intended to hold up the bar. It would be an insane action that even the most inexperienced hood would discard. There were half a dozen cops in the terminal corridor, some of them within yards of the bar. No, it was something else . . . but what?

He considered the possibility of immediately leaving the bar and putting distance between himself and the nervous man with the gun, and then decided that leaving a full drink on the counter would be more conspicuous. He paid for the drink, looked fixedly ahead, and sipped the martini without comment.

He was a careful man who kept his actions quietly unobtrusive, and although he had discarded the impulse to reject the lousy martini and leave, he shelved the feeling in a far compartment of his mind where it crouched unforgotten, but was held in check by the close control he always maintained. His body, which had momentarily tensed, began to relax. At the same time he automatically appraised the third man at the bar who clutched a thin briefcase as if it held something valuable. He reached across the counter for a pretzel with a glance that assimilated Lyon: tall, with sandy hair turning brown, and the eye lines of a smiling man. He wore a casual but expensive sport coat and slacks with scuffed shoes and mismatched socks. The man's invisible sensors retreated with a harmless verdict.

A rasping voice over the loudspeaker forced a long enunciation of vowels as it announced, "New England Express for Middleburg, Hartford, Springfield, and Bennington now loading at Gate Twenty-nine."

Willie Shep walked rapidly toward the corridor as the man with the beard picked up a small flight bag at his feet and followed. Lyon was last, and the three men were quickly lost from each other's view.

Willie Shep hurried and damned himself for that last beer. It was important that he board the bus first, and he nearly ran until his pace was broken by a uniformed policeman leaning against the wall directly in his path twirling his club by its leather thong. He crossed to the far side of the passageway and brushed against a diminutive man who cursed him in Spanish. Willie stopped and let his hand caress the hidden gun. The Puerto Rican's sneer faded as if he sensed some quality that stilled further aggression. He turned abruptly and hurried in the opposite direction.

Hate filled Willie Shep. Its tendrils radiated from him with a harshness that left a bitter residue. He wished that the weapon at his belt were a fully automatic rifle that he could level before him, turn to full fire, and cut a swath of death. He had considered that alternative for several days and nights as he lay on his narrow bed on East Tenth Street, but had finally settled on the plan he would now carry out.

It had started three weeks ago when they'd fired him from Miller's Supermarket. The manager had tried to con him into believing it was a "last on, first off" general layoff, but he knew better. The assistant manager, that bastard O'Halloran, was out to get him. That mick had hated his guts from the first day he'd reported for work—that was the real reason.

For the first week he hadn't been too pissed, in fact he was almost relieved to be released from the tedium of work; but then the unemployment compensation people started giving him a hard time. When he told them to take a flying fuck they told him that his claim would be indefinitely delayed. People loved screwing you, they got their jollies that way; just like Loyce had when he'd called and said his support money would be late.

"So, what else is new, Willie?" she had said. "Forget it. I've got an old man with balls who brings in bread regular." She'd laughed and hung up.

If he'd had the gun then he'd have given her a full clip right in the face. But he'd only had a few bucks, just enough to get tanked in a bar where some big bastard shot off his mouth. There had been a fight, and he'd been thrown out while the other patrons crowded in the doorway laughing.

He had waited until the plan was ready. A few more minutes and they wouldn't laugh again.

The man with the beard moved rapidly, but not in such a manner as to attract attention. His eyes darted from side to side scanning passing faces, checking, always checking. There was always the remote possibility that someone, some chance acquaintance might recognize him, wonder about his presence, and tuck the fact away for some future damaging use. It was that faint probability that could always spell disaster . . . and he was careful, as always.

Out of habit, Lyon bought a newspaper. He doubted that he'd read it during the two-and-a-half-hour trip, but held it as a possible security blanket against boredom. He took no note of others in the terminal, his mind still filled with benign monsters.

The short line before Gate 29 began to move through the door as Willie Shep pushed his way toward the front. The bus driver stood before the vehicle's open door and took the first ticket from a stout black woman. She boarded the bus and took the first seat by the window.

Willie shoved his ticket forward and received a disdainful glance as the driver reached past him and took the ticket from the next in line. Willie mashed his ticket into the driver's hand and stepped on the bus. He saw with relief that the seat immediately behind the driver's was empty. He slipped into it and sat on the outside to discourage occupancy by anyone else.

The man with the beard was ninth in line. His eyes swiveled across the bus and stopped for the briefest moment on Willie Shep before he walked briskly to the rear and took the last seat in front of the lavatory. The fact that the nervous man from the bar was on this bus nicked at him. It might require a change of plans, precautionary measures—care, always care, that was the secret. He leaned back in the seat with a low sigh.

Lyon Wentworth was the last to board. He found a vacant window seat near the rear of the bus, wedged his briefcase into the narrow space between seat and window, tilted his chair as far back as it would go, stretched out, and opened the newspaper. He felt a pleasant lassitude, as if he were on some remote beach with a warm sun on his face and soft wind brushing against his body. His eyes closed.

The driver stood facing the loaded bus with bobbing head and moving lips as he took a head count. He was a large black man dressed in well-creased navy-blue trousers and a white shirt with a narrow dark tie clasped between the second and third buttons. Finished counting, he waved to the dispatcher, sat behind the wheel, and hissed the door shut.

The engine started with a small vibration that shuddered through the bus. It backed slowly from the loading area, turned, and began to head down the exit ramp.

Willie Shep leaned toward the driver. "How long it take you to the tunnel?"

"About three months," the driver responded without turning.

"Don't smart ass me. The tunnel. The one down the street. What's it called?"

"The Lincoln Tunnel, and like I said, about three months. That's when I get transferred to another run."

"All the buses go through the tunnel. I watched for an hour yesterday. They all go through."

"Most do, but not this one."

"Over to Jersey."

"You got the right ticket on the wrong bus, mister." The bus reached the exterior of the building and paused for a light. "This is the New England Express: Hartford, Springfield, and up into Vermont. We go straight up Manhattan and catch the New England Thruway in the Bronx."

Willie Shep slipped the automatic from his waistband and placed the muzzle against the driver's ear. "I got a vote here that says we go through the tunnel."

"You drunk, mister?" The driver turned until he stared directly into the barrel of the gun. "You'll get in big trouble. Now put that thing away." The light changed and cars in the rear began to honk.

"The tunnel. Now!"

"You're the boss." The bus turned toward the access ramp of the Lincoln Tunnel as several passengers, familiar with the route, began to mumble.

"Keep going until I tell you to stop." Willie Shep stood in the front of the bus facing the passengers with the pistol, weaving slowly back and forth. He reached toward the driver with his free hand. "Give me the speaker."

The driver shook his head in resignation and handed the microphone from the side of the dashboard to Shep.

"Turn it on, damn it!" Willie again turned the gun toward the driver. "I said on, boy." His voice carried throughout the bus as the driver thumbed a switch. "I got a gun," Willie yelled, "and I can use

7

it." The anxiety in his voice pushed its register to within a few decibels of a screech. "Everyone stay put, shut up, and don't give me no trouble!"

The bearded man in the rear slouched deeper into his seat and tilted his cap further over his eyes. "Oh, shit," he mumbled softly.

Lyon Wentworth jerked awake. He had unconsciously pulled the newspaper across his chest as if it were a bed sheet warding off an intruder. For a moment the rapid change of milieu disoriented him, and it took a few seconds for his eyes to focus on the slender man at the front of the bus waving the gun. The obvious danger in the situation tensed his body and dispelled the aura of well-being.

Were they always the same, these unspectacular men? Twisted, warped, with radiating bitterness that moved in pulsating rings, withering all in their paths?

The heavy black woman in the seat adjacent to the driver began to scream.

"Shut up!"

She continued screaming.

Willie turned toward the driver as the bus began the final approach to the tunnel. "Stop this thing and open the door."

"Yes, sir." The driver responded with an alacrity that obviously indicated he was under the impression that his unwelcome passenger was departing. The bus stopped with a jerk that threw the passengers forward in their seats. The door hissed open.

"I told you to be quiet."

She screamed again.

He raised the automatic and shot her twice in the face. Her head lurched backward against the window. Grabbing her arm, he jockeyed her forward and let her fall through the door to tumble onto the pavement in a pool of rushing blood.

"Get going."

Willie Shep stood by the driver, holding on to a vertical pole with one hand, while the other arched the automatic back and forth as the bus moved into the tunnel. The passengers sat in numb shock, the only sound that of the engine and *whish* of tires on pavement.

An old woman in the fifth row clutched a knitting bag to her body with talonlike fingers. The noise she made was nearly inaudible at first, but as the litany continued, its increased intensity made it clear to everyone. "Put it down . . . put it down. . . ." The old woman's chant was rhythmic as it increased in volume.

"Stop it, grandma."

"Put it down . . . put it down. . . ." She seemed oblivious to him as he moved down the aisle. He stopped by the fifth seat and placed the gun against her forehead. She continued staring ahead and making the low moaning sounds. The driver glanced apprehensively in the rear-view mirror as the other passengers, as if a single organism, took a simultaneous intake of breath.

"You're next, grandma."

She slowly turned toward him. "I am going to see my grandchildren in Vermont."

"Rush the bastard!" A young man, wearing an Adidas T-shirt, sprang from his seat and lunged toward Shep. A shot tore into his arm and knocked him to the floor.

Willie Shep retreated to the front of the bus. "Anyone else moves gets it. Understand!" He glanced to the front. "We're halfway through the tunnel. Stop the bus."

The bus slowed to a gradual halt with its nose just before the wide stripe at the tunnel's midpoint that divides New York from New Jersey. The driver switched on the emergency flashers and lowered his head across his arms spread on the steering wheel.

Cars behind them began to ease slowly into the vacant left lane, and then that too ceased, and they were alone in the deserted tunnel. It became apparent to Lyon that Transit Authority police had now sealed both ends of the tunnel. A protective sheath was beginning to enclose them. There would be hurried conferences, a marshaling of forces coordinated on both sides of the river, and then a gradual movement toward them.

The bus began to move again. Slowly, directed by whispered commands from the hijacker, it backed, turned, and backed again until it slanted across both lanes. The engine died again, and only the center aisle lights illuminated the shadowy, stricken faces of the passengers.

Lyon realized the hijacker's strategy. With the bus astride the tunnel, he had a clear view of both the front and rear approaches, while his flanks were protected by the walls of the tunnel.

Willie gestured to the young man on the floor who clutched his wounded arm. "You! On your feet. You're the messenger."

9

Hands reached into the aisle and helped him struggle to his feet. "What do you want me to do?"

"What's your name?"

"Hannon. Robert Hannon."

"Okay, Bob, baby. You take the news out of here." Willie found that he was beginning to enjoy the situation. It had all gone as planned. All the things he had thought of those nights on the bed at East Tenth Street had come to pass. So, he had to shoot the fat one —just as well. Someone had to be made an example of. "Listen, Bobby. You get off the bus and walk back the way we came. Pretty soon you'll come to cops, right?"

"I suppose."

"You tell them what's happened. You tell them that there's a real mean son of a bitch here who's already killed once, shot you, and has got a dozen buddies in the Freedom Army helping him. You tell them they got one hour to get a million bucks in hundred-dollar bills back on this bus—carried by you. Got that?"

"A million in hundreds."

"And more. Tell them I want a jet on the runway at Newark Airport with parachutes. And no cops near the plane or my buddies will set off the bombs in the terminal. Got that?"

"A jet with parachutes. Bombs in the terminal."

"And they got one hour. One hour or I start killing people. I kill someone for every five minutes they're late. Got that?"

"You start killing people," Robert Hannon repeated numbly.

"Get going. Fast—or I get somebody else and leave you dead."

The young man, still clutching his wounded arm, stumbled painfully down the aisle. He glanced once at Willie Shep and then went out the door.

Willie glanced at the nonexistent watch on his wrist and let out a low curse. He had pawned it, and now wouldn't know when the hour was up, much less the five-minute increments. What the hell. He laughed. There were eighteen passengers including the driver left on the bus, and probably as many watches. Not that he wanted a woman's watch, but there would be others. He glanced at the driver who was still hunched over the wheel with his arms spread. He wore a large chronometer-type watch with several dials and a sweep second hand. "Gimme the watch."

"What?" The driver looked up at Willie with a slow confused movement.

"You heard me. The watch."

"You want my wallet too?" He slipped the band off his wrist and gingerly handed it over.

"Get to the back of the bus."

As the driver made his way down the aisle, Willie turned to peer out the window. A hundred yards in front he could see two police cars, with blinking roof lights, pulled across the roadway. Other cars, ambulances, and tow trucks were behind the automobile barricade. He looked out the other side and saw the scene repeated. He sat down on the floor with his feet stretched forward and the gun held in both hands.

His planning had been excellent, he thought with satisfaction. The narrow tunnel gave him protection on both sides. Any attempt to storm the bus would have to be either from the front or rear, and he'd take five passengers with him if they tried that. He looked at the watch. It was five. He'd start counting off the five-minute intervals exactly at six. He smiled. It had begun.

The whispering voice near Lyon's ear was nearly toneless. The man behind him had leaned forward until his lips were only inches from the narrow aperture between the seats. His droning whisper was far too low for the hijacker at the front of the bus to hear.

"He's a nut," the voice said. "There will be more killing."

"The police will do something." Lyon found himself whispering through clenched teeth.

"Sure they will. But some of us won't be here to see it."

"They've stopped this kind of thing before. They have special teams to handle it."

"They've been lucky. This time they won't be. You saw what happened when the kid tried to rush him. This guy'll kill four, maybe six, more."

"There's nothing we can do." There was a pronounced edge of fear in Lyon's voice.

"Maybe there is."

Lyon looked up the aisle to where the hijacker sat on the floor. His profile was well below the window line and protected from police sharpshooters. What did they do in cases like this? Talk the man out?

11

Rush him? Yes, there had been a good deal of that lately. Percussion grenades combined with overpowering firepower and a quick dash by special teams who hoped to move fast enough to save most of the passengers. Most of them . . .

He leaned back with the newspaper crushed between his hands, and tilted his head toward the aperture between the seats. "Any ideas?"

"You ever in the army?"

"Long time ago. Korea."

"Fired a weapon?"

"Well, yes, but . . ."

"You have a newspaper. I saw it. Hold it over the space between the seats." The voice was low and commanding.

Lyon held the newspaper over the aperture and felt something metal thrust into his hand. He glanced down to see that he held the barrel of a large revolver. He automatically reversed the weapon until the butt rested in his palm and his finger curled over the trigger guard.

"Kill him," the voice behind him whispered.

"I can't do that." His voice was a hoarse whisper.

"You have to."

"Take this back." He tried to force the gun through the seat opening, but felt unyielding pressure, probably the man's knees pressed against the opening.

I was an intelligence officer, he wanted to say. I never fired at the enemy. But he had once. . . . One quiet night he had gone to the division Ranger Company's forward position to debrief a patrol that had returned to their lines. He was hunched over in a bunker with a pad on his knees when it started. Loud bugles . . . noise . . . so much noise, and then the searchlights reflecting off low-hanging clouds as they all rushed to the parapet. He'd automatically grabbed his M-2 carbine, switched it to full fire, and was on his second clip when a large hand pressed against his shoulder.

"You're blowing away our defensive wire, Captain," Rocco Herbert, the Ranger commanding officer, had said. "Please open your eyes."

Again, long ago, he had fired at a man with his eyes open. The vision still haunted him and peopled his dreams with a guilt that no rationalization could remove.

"I won't be able to do it," he said aloud.

"What's going on back there?" The hijacker stood in a crouch and aimed his weapon toward the rear of the bus. "You hear me? What's going on? Answer me!"

Lyon tensed. His hand holding the large revolver perspired against the cool metal. He pushed back against the cushions.

"You going to answer me?" Willie Shep's voice cracked in an adolescent quaver as it reached the top range of its register. "You . . . second from the toilet." The gun pointed directly at Lyon. "Yes, you, buddy boy. Stand up, motherfucker."

"I'm not doing anything," Lyon said in a low voice. He wondered if his words carried to the front of the bus. His hand was moist as it gripped the revolver, his finger refusing to curl around the trigger. He tried to remember long ago days in the army. The gun he held was large, probably a .44 Magnum. Would its characteristics be different from the standard army .45? He remembered days on the pistol range when he had fired the bucking .45 . . . and his inability to hit anything.

The humane action would be to shoot the hijacker in a nonfatal part of the body . . . perhaps the shoulder, the projectile numbing his gun arm and throwing him backward into a position where they could easily overpower him. Realizing his lack of expertise with a handgun, he felt he'd probably miss and possibly even kill one of the other passengers. They must wait. The police would eventually make their move. They'd storm the bus and the passengers could throw themselves to the floor and hope.

"I hate your kind, motherfucker." The hijacker's voice dropped to a lower and more menacing tone as he hunched down the aisle toward Lyon. "I know your kind. You fill your goddamn shopping carts with martini olives and cheese, and when you can't find something you ask me and never even see me. You make me put your crap in bags, and you never know who I am. Things are different now. I'm the man here, and you better look at me good. Hear me?"

"I hear you," Lyon said and was surprised at the evenness of his voice.

"You're going to kiss my feet, baby. And if you're real lucky, I might not blow your head off." Willie Shep was now one seat away with the gun pointed directly at Lyon's head. His eyes glinted with odd flaking specks that Lyon had observed once before when a student in one of his classes had inexplicably and without warning thrown a desk chair through a second-story window.

"On the floor." The automatic wavered two feet from Lyon.

All further internal arguments regarding accuracy with weapons were now academic, but he knew if he left his seat to follow the hijacker's commands that the gun in his lap would be revealed and he would be shot.

"You got three seconds."

Instant calculations: if he propelled himself upward directly at the hijacker . . . the .32 clenched a few feet from him was a small-caliber gun, and unless it hit a vital organ . . . his alternatives were tantamount to self-destruction. He had two options, one only slightly more acceptable than the other. "All right," he murmered and half stood.

A small smile curled along the edge of Willie Shep's face at the instant Lyon fired the Magnum through the newspaper.

The entrance wound of the soft-nosed projectile with an impact of 1,310 foot pounds was upward through the left eye. The bullet exited through the crown of the head and continued through the roof of the bus to ricochet off the tunnel ceiling.

The screams of the passengers began before the massive reverberation of the shot had ceased echoing.

2 The gun fell from Lyon's limp hand and clattered across the flooring. He stood with stunned shock staring down at the body sprawled obscenely across the aisle. And then, instinctively, he knelt next to the distorted body in a vain attempt to aid, to keep vital forces alive, anything to maintain life's spark in the man he had just shot.

It was apparent that the hijacker was dead.

He heard a short choking cry and at first thought it came from up the aisle, and then knew it was himself. He retreated from the corpse with a backward splaying motion and looked down at his hands and the front of his jacket where blood of the slain man stained in Rorschach splotches. He ripped the coat from his shoulders and threw it in a wadded ball.

He was alone in the bus and watched with detachment as uniformed -men carrying rifles and wearing bulky flack vests rushed from the distant barricades.

The other passengers had scurried from the bus like flushed quail, and now hovered near the door as if hidden in some safe thicket. The emergency door immediately behind him swung slowly to and fro.

Peristaltic waves rippled his stomach until they dredged up bile that

15

he vomited on the flooring. It coated the pointed tips of the dead man's boots, and he turned away to retch and buried his head on his arms across a seat top.

Wary men, clutching rifles, began silently to enter the bus and move toward him.

"You the one who shot him."

It seemed more a statement than a question. He brushed beads of perspiration from his forehead and tried to focus his eyes and thoughts. "Yes," he finally managed to say.

A hand on his shoulder. "Come on, buddy. Outa' here into some clean air."

Other hands . . . helping him out the emergency door. A knot of passengers ahead, fingers pointed in his direction. Another hand grasped his elbow, propelled him along the tunnel to where a police car waited with open door and flashing roof light.

Men in mufti broke through the police cordon and ran toward him. Several dropped into a crouch and strobe lights flickered. They began to surround him with shouted questions until the officer holding his arm waved them away.

A thin black woman passenger, her face still elongated with fear, grasped at him. "You are the One. I saw you in the cards this morning."

He was pushed into the rear of the cruiser and the door slammed. Faces pressed against the window, a microphone was stuck against the wire mesh separating the front and rear seats.

"You shot him?" an insistent voice asked.

"Blew the fucker's head off," a heavy cop said as he pushed the radio interviewer away and sat in the front seat.

"How does it feel?"

"Terrible," he mumbled.

"Your name . . . where you from? . . . what sort of gun? . . . shot him where? . . . he fire back? . . . you a peace officer?" The battery of shouted questions seemed to bounce inside the car's interior until the whole world became an accusatory thing.

The door next to Lyon opened and a detective, his badge on the outside of his jacket, swung inside and cocked a finger at the driver. The car moved slowly through the crowd, parting waves of reluctant reporters in its path.

16

As the cruiser slowly passed a knot of officers, both in uniform and out, it paused briefly to allow a barricading vehicle to be moved. Lyon looked out the window and found himself staring at a bearded man in a sport coat with a gold badge hanging from his breast pocket. The face was familiar, and then the man turned away and the car continued on.

Light engulfed them as they moved from the tunnel into midtown Manhattan. The driver flipped on the siren and its wail opened a passage through traffic.

"You okay?" the detective by his side asked.

"I was sick back there, but I think I'm all right now. Can we open a window?"

"Don't open back here. You're not hurt or anything?"

"He didn't touch me."

The detective chuckled. "A few more like you and there won't be more of that shit. What'd you shoot him with? A cannon?"

"I don't know. It was a big gun."

The cop looked at him quizzically and then turned away with a shrug. "We'll talk about it when we get to the office."

"I think I'd like to stop for a drink."

"Sure, buddy. Just a few formalities and we'll get you tanked."

"Uh huh."

"Say, what's your name?"

"Wentworth. Lyon Wentworth."

"Okay, Lyon. You're the man of the hour. Hell, yes." He glanced out the rear window at the *Daily News* radio car to their rear. "We'll try and keep the reporters away from you until you feel like facing them."

They parked in a reserved space in front of an official-looking building where Lyon was bustled up a short set of steps. More photographers snapped pictures and another microphone was thrust in his face. The guiding detective pushed it away and then they were inside.

More bedlam. Officers crowded around and two reporters had managed to reach the inner recess of the building.

"Hey, Harry. I heard the mayor's coming down to thank this guy."

"After we check things out," the detective replied as a girdling group of cops took Lyon into the elevator. They left the elevator on the fourth floor and exited into a large squad room where shirt-sleeved detectives looked at Lyon and his escort with open curiosity. A second elevator opened behind them to disgorge more bus passengers and police.

The thin black woman pressed through the crowd and plucked at Lyon's sleeve. "You are a hungan. A hungan filled with lao."

They tried to propel Lyon forward, but he jerked away and turned to her. "You're Haitian?"

"Not for many years, but I do not forget."

"What's she talking about?" the detective called Harry asked.

"She follows the god of Vodun," Lyon said and took the woman's hand in his. "We're sorry it happened," he said softly.

"It had to be."

"What in Christ's name is she talking about?"

Lyon left the black woman and followed the detectives. "Voodoo."

"Jesus H. Christ! That's all we need in Manhattan West."

They went down a short hallway that entered into a large private office with an imitation Persian rug on the floor and functional furnishings. Harry opened an inner door to a small bathroom and gestured. "Case you want to wash off or something."

"Thanks." Lyon shut and latched the door before placing both hands on the sink and bending over the bowl. He remained immobile for several moments trying to assimilate the rush of events that had cracked the veneer of his life. When he looked up, he saw his reflection in the narrow mirror. A small muscle in his lower jaw quivered under his red eyes and drawn facial lines.

He shook his head and splashed water on his face as the mirror image dissolved to be replaced by one of the hijacker standing in the bus aisle. The gun extended, the cracked smile grimaced, and again Lyon clutched the large gun under the newspaper and watched the hole erupt in the man's face.

He turned from the mirror with the after-image still scorching his mind.

He washed his hands for a long time without looking up, and then went back into the office.

The dramatis personae had changed. A different group turned to face him in silent tableau. In the far corner, as unobtrusive as possible, a prim policewoman sat with fingers poised over a stenographic machine. On the small leather divan a large man with a heavily jowled face, tailored business suit, and short hair looked at Lyon with a lopsided grin.

A man of Lyon's age behind the desk seemed to have grown from the furniture. His arms extended forward along its empty surface while his head, large and out of proportion to the remainder of his body, was dominated by heavy bushy eyebrows.

"Wentworth," the man behind the desk snapped at Lyon in more of a command than a salutation. "I'm Nesbitt. Captain." He moved one arm in an almost imperceptible wave toward the policewoman in the corner. "Officer Hayes." His arm resumed its former position. "And as if you couldn't tell, the other gentleman is Special Agent McAllister from the local field office."

McAllister gave a nonchalant wave. "Feel up to a few questions?"

"I guess so." He took a seat in a side chair placed directly in the center between the two men.

"Anything I can get you?"

"No, thank you. Unless you have some Dry Sack."

"No sherry, but we keep the snakebite medicine handy." He took a bottle of bourbon from the bottom desk drawer, cracked the seal, and poured two stiff fingers in a water tumbler.

Lyon sank back in the chair after accepting the whiskey. He held the glass with both hands, took a long sip, and felt the liquor traverse his body in a warm snaking motion. He took another sip and found that both men were staring at him, without hostility, but perhaps as individuals observing an interesting specimen. "Why the FBI?"

"Our mad friend took the bus over a state line and made bomb threats."

"No, I don't think so," Lyon replied. "If that stripe they have in the tunnel is correct, we were still in New York."

"A technicality. We think the kid he sent with the ransom demand crossed the line."

"Were any bombs found?"

"None."

"Be that as it will," Nesbitt said, "it seems to us, Wentworth, that the city of New York and sixteen bus passengers owe you a vote of thanks."

"It was an accident. What I mean is, I had no choice. Did you say sixteen people?"

The two law enforcement officers glanced at each other. "You watch the details, don't you? Sixteen if we don't count you and do count the driver. We're grateful. In fact, the mayor and commissioner very well might come down to offer you their personal thanks on behalf of the city. As soon as we sweep up a few minor details."

"Wait a minute." Lyon put the liquor glass down on the desk. "I believe there were eighteen left alive on the bus, including me."

"You shot one."

"Besides that. Doesn't one of the passengers wear a beard? He also had on a cap, a jacket of some light material. Medium build, thirty-ish?"

Captain Nesbitt made rapid notes on a small pad. "I'll check on it."

"It could be significant."

"By the way—and I'm praying for luck on this one—do you have a permit for your gun?"

"It wasn't mine."

"It wasn't yours," McAllister repeated in a drone. "Whose was it?"

"I don't know."

"You don't know," Nesbitt repeated in a sad sort of way. He looked down at his pad for a few moments. "Okay, from there. What did you do with the gun?"

"I dropped it on the floor."

Nesbitt immediately pressed a button on his phone, picked up the receiver, and talked quietly for a few moments. "Call me back at once." He hung up. "Okay, let's start it from the top. Sorry to bother you with all this, considering what you've been through, but all the passengers will go through it. We'll make it as painless as possible."

"I can understand."

"Your name is Lyon Wentworth. Address?"

"R.D. Two, Murphysville, Connecticut." He watched the police-woman's fingers nimbly flick across the steno machine. He'd have to look into the mechanism of those things sometime.

"You're employed, Mr. Wentworth?"

"I am self-employed."

"As what?"

"I'm a writer."

"Oh, really." McAllister and Nesbitt exchanged looks as if this

20

information had some significance that was lost to Lyon. "Have you written anything I might know?"

"Not unless you have children."

"Matter of fact, I do."

"Well, my book *The Cat in the Capitol* did quite well. Then there was *Nancy Goes to Mount Vernon,* and the Wobbly series has had a rather modest success."

McAllister leaned forward with both hands on his knees. *"Nancy Goes to Mount Vernon?"*

"Not my usual thing, but they wanted something like that for the Bicentennial."

Nesbitt glanced at the stenographer again before looking back to Lyon. "Wife's name?"

"Secretary Beatrice Wentworth."

Nesbitt shrugged. "We don't need her occupation." He paused and then asked Lyon quietly, "Secretary of what?"

"The state of Connecticut."

"Oh, my God!" McAllister slouched back in the couch.

"Am I to understand that your wife is Secretary of State?"

"Secretary of the State . . . for Connecticut."

"Yes, of course. Sorry." Nesbitt thought a moment and then looked at McAllister. "Why didn't we call in sick this morning?"

"I was just thinking that Wentworth might be right," McAllister said as he stood. "That bus was on the New York side of the line and . . ."

"Sit down," Nesbitt ordered. "The kid carried the demands across the line."

"Technical point."

"Start from the top, Wentworth. The whole day."

"I left Murphysville at six this morning and caught the seven A.M. bus from Middleburg. I arrived in the city at nine-thirty, had breakfast, and went to my publisher's office."

"Where's that?"

"On Madison Avenue. We had a conference, lunch, and then I walked to the bus terminal. I was a little early, so I stopped in a small bar to have a drink."

"How many of what?"

"One of what I'm not sure."

"You remember the exact number of people on the bus, but not what you had to drink? Then?"

"They announced the bus at Gate Twenty-nine. I boarded last, I believe."

"Where did you sit?"

"In the rear." Lyon continued recounting the events that even in this short time span had taken on an aura of unreality. They let him proceed without further interruption. ". . . and I was there, by the body, when the police came in. And that's it."

They looked at him skeptically. The stenographer stopped the dance of her fingers and kept her head down over the small machine.

"This man gave you—the man in the seat behind you—gave you the gun?"

"That's correct."

"Why did he do that? Why didn't he use it himself?"

"How would I know?" A note of peevishness crept into his voice, and he realized he was tired, very tired. The emotionalism of the last hour had drained him, and he wanted nothing more than sleep.

"Do people often give you guns to hold, sir?" the FBI agent asked in a low voice.

"I'm not sure I care for that remark." Lyon faced the agent who had folded his arms across his chest.

"About the gun," Nesbitt said. "After you fired, you dropped it on the floor."

"That's right."

"Do you know what kind it was?"

"Big. A forty-four Magnum, I'd say."

"You could hardly put a gun of that size in an ordinary pocket. I'll be right back." Nesbitt left the room and McAllister leaned toward Lyon.

"You know, Wentworth, you can level with us. We'll see that you're protected. What I'm trying to say is, after what you did, no one is going to prosecute you on a gun-carrying charge. You're from out of state, probably unaware of New York law. Or how about your wife fixing it so you have a back-dated permit?"

"It wasn't my gun."

Nesbitt returned and slammed the door. He moved in jerky motions as a muscle in the side of his face twitched. "They can't find the goddamn weapon. They've lost the goddamn piece!"

"That's impossible."

"We have the hijacker's gun, but no Magnum."

"It could have been kicked under the seat."

He glared at Lyon. "We searched the bus."

"I told you, I dropped it on the floor. I didn't want any part of it."

Nesbitt beckoned. "I want you to identify some items."

They returned to the squad room where the other passengers were being interviewed at desks lined in neat, ordered rows. A long table under the windows was covered with a multitude of tagged items. There were shopping bags, suitcases, newspapers, and an assortment of hand-carried luggage that had rested on the rack inside the bus or been found on seats or the floor. Lyon walked the length of the table until stopping near the far end where he picked up his briefcase and showed it to Captain Nesbitt. "This is mine."

"May we open it?"

"Why?" He found himself on the verge of belligerency.

"Routine."

"Go ahead. I have nothing to hide."

Nesbitt handed the case to an aide who took it to a desk where he methodically searched and made an inventory of the contents. Lyon continued scanning the assortment spread on the table and gingerly picked up an automatic pistol encased in an acetate bag. "This looks like the weapon the hijacker was carrying, but I couldn't swear to it."

"We think it is."

Two items next to the gun interested him: a poplin jacket and a small flight bag. "The man who gave me the gun—I think he was wearing a jacket like this. Now that I think about it, I believe he was sitting next to me in the bar and had a bag like this near the stool."

Nesbitt glanced at the tags on the jacket and bag. "They were found on the floor of the last seat." He looked thoughtful. "It's possible that the guy in the last seat took these off, put on something he had in the bag, and left—after picking up the gun."

"It could have been a sport coat." Lyon had a fleeting recall picture of a man in a sport jacket and beard standing in the tunnel as the

23

police cruiser slowly rolled past. "As we were leaving the tunnel, I saw a man in a jacket, wearing a gold badge, who might have been the man behind me."

"A cop?"

"He had a badge hanging from his pocket."

"Let's go back to my office."

They resumed their places in the office, although Nesbitt, for reasons of his own, had dismissed the stenographer. The captain sat behind his desk and drummed his fingers. "Are you sure it was the same guy?"

"No, but it could have been."

"A cop . . . a gold badge . . . but why not use the gun himself, why give it to you?"

"I don't know, Captain. All I can tell you is what happened."

"That was an interstate bus," McAllister said. "Do your men usually carry their weapons when they cross state lines?"

"Not unless they're on official business. That's why I'm very interested in the guy—if he is a cop."

"I can only tell you what I saw. The man who sat behind me and gave me the gun is possibly the man I later saw in the tunnel with a badge."

"And you'd know him?"

"I don't think identification of that sort can ever be absolute."

"As you can imagine, the situation interests us."

"Right now I want to get out of here and go home."

"I'd like you to look at some photographs, Mr. Wentworth."

"Now?"

"We know you've been through an ordeal. Could you come back in the morning? The bus company is providing facilities for everyone involved."

"Yes, of course." Lyon wondered if they'd be quite so considerate if it weren't for his wife's position.

"Missing gun or not," Nesbitt said as he crossed the room and extended his hand, "we still thank you."

The detective called Harry took Lyon in an unmarked car to an East Side hotel where the Nutmeg Transportation Company had rented a floor. As they left the elevator on the sixth floor, they found themselves in a large foyer where a bar had been set up and a uniformed bartender mixed drinks.

The other passengers had arrived a few minutes before and had drinks in hand as they talked in a loud chatter. As the elevator door closed behind Harry and Lyon, the room grew silent while everyone turned toward them.

Lyon gave a small wave and then whispered to Harry. "Do you know where my room is?"

"Sure." He led Lyon midway down the hall to an open door. When the detective entered, he checke·ʾ the window to make sure it was locked and looked into the bathroom and single closet. "You're in with a guy named Collins."

Lyon glanced at a new valise aligned neatly on the luggage rack at the head of one of the twin beds, and then over to the far bed where his briefcase had been thrown. He watched Harry continue his minute search of the room. "Are you worried or something?"

"The city of New York wants that nothing happens to you."

"That's reassuring."

"Should be. There'll be two of us on the floor all night."

"Fine."

The detective left and Lyon sank onto the bed. His life had been changed, and he wondered if the afternoon's events could ever be set aside. A lethargy consumed him, and he wanted to lie on the bed, close his eyes, and fall into an oblivious sleep.

He must call Bea.

The prospect of any well-meaning friend calling his wife and informing her of the day's events horrified him. Or she might turn on the news. . . . He must get to her first.

He reached for the bedside phone and asked the operator for his Connecticut number.

The phone rang . . . rang . . . and rang.

3 Bea Wentworth had never become accustomed to hate. The strength of voters' feelings often seemed to transcend ordinary political differences. Not only did they disapprove of her positions, they often acted as if she were personally endeavoring to overthrow the Republic single-handedly. The loyalty of her supporters nurtured her career and allowed her usually to succeed in November, but she sometimes felt that her supporters did not have the fervor of her enemies—or at least that's the way it seemed.

The Murphysville High School auditorium was only one-third filled, but this did not discourage the zeal of the moderator. At least she thought it was zeal. The batteries on her hearing aid were weak, and sound had begun to drift toward the inaudible range. She reached for the tiny device in her ear, twisted the volume to its loudest position, and once again the words were discernible.

The moderator nodded toward Bea on his right and then toward her opponent on his left. "And now that we've had the formal presentations from our congressional candidates, we move into what I call 'cross fire,' which is when they direct questions at each other."

Bea smiled with affection as she saw Rocco Herbert at the rear of the auditorium yawn in a losing battle to stay awake. Rocco, Murphysville's chief of police and Lyon's best friend, had uncomfortably folded his six-foot-eight frame and 280 pounds into the last seat in the rear row.

"Our first question, determined by a flip of a coin earlier, goes to Willard Morris."

Bea snapped her attention back to the dais. Her opponent nodded in her direction and was about to begin when an aide whispered and slipped him a note. Willard Morris glanced over at Bea with a smile she could only categorize as malevolent. Still, he was good-looking, and like so many young Turks who now filled the political scene, he seemed cloned from the depths of some public relations firm. The qualifications did not seem to improve over the old machine ward heelers; at least the machine men were known to represent certain vested interests. The new ones disguised their leanings, blew in the wind, and this one was about to blow at her—with both barrels.

"Madam Secretary"—he made it sound derogatory—"your stand on gun control legislation is well known. In fact, when you were state senator from this district, you introduced the first such bill, even with the knowledge that Connecticut, the arsenal of democracy, has a good many residents employed by gun manufacturers. However, I would like your explanation as to how you reconcile that position with your husband's possession of a loaded gun in New York City this afternoon?"

Rocco Herbert snapped awake and stood in the aisle.

"I'm sorry," Bea answered. "I don't understand the question."

"I'm referring to your husband shooting a man today."

"I'm sure my opponent is mistaken," Bea said to the moderator.

"Would you please clarify that, Mr. Morris?"

Willard Morris waved his note in the air. "It has been announced that Lyon Wentworth of Murphysville, Connecticut, shot a man in the Lincoln Tunnel today."

There were murmurs throughout the audience as all eyes turned toward Bea.

"Unless there's another Lyon Wentworth around here," Willard Morris added quickly.

Bea saw Rocco leave the auditorium. The increasing noise from the audience was lost as the hearing aid lapsed into silence. Her voice unconsciously rose. "YOU KNOW, WILLARD, YOU'VE SAID SOME DUMB THINGS IN THESE DEBATES, BUT THAT'S THE DUMBEST AND LOWEST YET. IF YOU'LL EXCUSE ME." She rushed for the steps at the side of the stage and ran up the side aisle after Rocco.

She found him at a pay phone down the corridor near the cafeteria. He hung up as she reached him. "It seems to be true, Bea. God only knows how. Last time I saw Lyon fire a weapon was in Korea when he blew away half our defensive wire."

"IT CAN'T BE. He's incapable of hurting anyone."

"Let's go to the office and get the details."


When Lyon entered the cocktail party in the wide foyer, all conversation came to an abrupt halt. They turned to face him, drinks in hand, the festive mood switching to awe. He remembered only a few of them: the thin voodoo lady, the crooning grandmother now incongruously holding a large manhattan cocktail, a short bespectacled man with thinning hair, the others a blur of vague remembrances.

They were the usual assortment of individuals who seem to ride long distance buses, but were now fused together by a common experience that would forever weld their lives. He had heard people tell of such cohesion in the Underground tunnels of London during the blitz and by men in combat units who shared a common hell unknown to others.

Half of the passengers were black, who perhaps rode buses for economic reasons; another quarter seemed to be older women on their way to visit relatives; servicemen and commuter types like Lyon made up the remainder of the group.

Lyon smiled and they relaxed. "Do you suppose he's got a sherry back there?"

The mood broke as they swirled around him with voices that merged into incoherence. A large glass was shoved in his hand as he listened and nodded.

The elevator doors opened and again the crowd quieted. Robert Hannon, the young man who had been shot, stood before them with his arm in a sling. He waved with his uninjured arm. "They said I could go home. Lucky for me he didn't have Mr. Wentworth's gun or I wouldn't have an arm."

They made a tight circle around Lyon and the young man.

"Everyone listen a minute." A rotund man with a round cherry face stood on a chair. "I'm Joe Moultrie and advertising gimmicks is my game: matchbooks, golf tees, that sort of thing."

"We don't want any." There was more good-natured jeering.

"Wait a sec. I'm not selling tonight, at least not my usual line. Now, I think that we've all been through something today." There was mutual agreement. "And I think we ought to make this an annual occasion. A get-together. You know, a reunion right here, this room, this date, next year. What do you say?"

There was unanimous approval.

Lyon felt a tap on his shoulder and turned toward a very sincere-looking bus driver. "I'm the one who should really thank you, Mr. Wentworth."

Lyon shook his head. "I'd rather you didn't."

"They wanted to give me a week off with pay, but I talked them into letting me take the special bus tomorrow morning. No other passengers but those of us here, plus a good-looking hostess to serve coffee and rolls. Real class, but the folks deserve it."

"I think they do."

At eight they were ceremoniously ushered into a private dining room at the end of the hall. There was momentary confusion over the seating arrangements until the driver took the place at the head of the table. Lyon found himself facing a wilted fruit cocktail with the voodoo lady to one side and a short man with thinning hair on the other.

During the introductions, he discovered that the black woman was Maura Dalencourt, a Haitian who had moved to New York thirty years ago and worked, until her retirement, as a chambermaid for the Plaza Hotel. She talked to Lyon with extreme deference, her eyes never leaving his, as if she still felt him possessed with divine power.

"I understand we're roommates, Mr. Wentworth."

Lyon turned to the man seated at his right. "Mr. Collins?"

"Yes. Major Collins, U.S. Army, retired." The handshake was limp, the palm sweaty. "Don't worry, Mr. Wentworth, I don't have any combat nightmares and wake up screaming. Thirty years in the Finance Corps never put me within a hundred miles of any shooting.

I'm traveling on a thirty-day ticket and plan to spend a week in New England. I wonder if you could suggest some points of interest I might take in?"

It happened as they were finishing the prime rib entrée.

Maura Dalencourt stood with a sharp cry and raked her cheeks with clawlike fingers. Her choking sounds were nearly incoherent. "The duppy! The duppy of the evil one is here!"

Lyon clutched her hand. "It's all right, Maura. It's all right."

"There is the sign of the duppy!" She pointed a thin finger toward the center of the table where a fork and butter knife lay crossed over each other.

"No, it's going to be all right." Lyon put his arm around her and led her from the room toward a small alcove in the foyer. They sat on a narrow love seat with their knees touching. He put his hands over hers. "There is no duppy. The man is dead and the duppy gone."

"You know of the soul, you know he was Baron Samedi, the evil one."

"I know you are safe."

"Because you see such things you are a good Rada, the one who killed Petro the evil one."

"I am concerned—for you."

"It is unusual for a white man to be aware of this."

"I read many books."

Her hands left his and vibrated before them. "I feel it. The duppy wills us to die."

"No," Lyon said softly. "I do not feel that. We are all tired from the day, that is all." He brought her hands back to her lap and felt the pressure of her squeeze. He wondered how many times in the past he might have passed her in the halls of the Plaza, how many times she might have come into his room unnoticed.

"I will be all right?"

"I promise you." She sighed, and the very structure of her body relaxed as tension seeped from her hand to his. Her head nodded, her eyes closed, and she leaned against his shoulder and slept.

Later, two of the other women passengers led the barely conscious Maura Dalencourt to her room. Lyon stretched and tried to work out the stiffness caused by the long uncomfortable position on the narrow love seat. They told him he had a phone call.

He took it in his room and held the phone away from his ear. "ARE YOU ALL RIGHT, LYON?"

"I wasn't hurt."

"THANK GOD FOR THAT. It took some doing, but Rocco finally got through to Captain Nesbitt, who told us the whole story. We'll pick you up in less than three hours."

"Wait until morning. I'm about ready for bed now and have to look at some photographs in the morning."

"We'll meet you in Nesbitt's office. And, Lyon—I love you."

"I love you too, Bea." He knew she was searching for more to say, something that would make it all right, but of course the phrases could not be found. It didn't matter, he knew what she meant. "Good night, darling," he finally said.

"Good night," she answered, and there wasn't any necessity to say more.

"Mr. Wentworth."

The soft tone startled him and he turned quickly to face the door.

"Oh, Major Collins, you gave me a start."

"I'm sorry, sir. Thought you might like a nightcap. Sherry, isn't it?" He extended a glass.

"Yes, thank you."

"Do you think there's anything to the old woman's demons and curses?"

"Good Lord, no."

He sat on the edge of his bed. "I thought I knew you from somewhere, so I hope you don't mind that I asked that we bunk together?"

"No, of course not. Please call me Lyon, or, in fact, anything you want as long as it's not Baron Samedi."

"Samedi?"

"A voodoo bad guy." Lyon pulled on his drink. "That one's not in my two-oh-one file."

"Two-oh-one file?"

Lyon detected the vague trace of an accent in his companion's voice, but couldn't place the country of origin.

"What can I do for you?"

Collins extended a copy of Lyon's book, *The Wobblies' Revenge.* "I'm going to stop and see my grandson in Springfield, and I bought it this morning. You are the author, aren't you?"

31

Lyon glanced at his photograph on the back of the dust jacket and smiled at Collins. "I plead guilty."

"If it's not too much trouble, I wonder if you'd autograph it for me?"

"Of course." Lyon accepted the pen and opened the book to the flyleaf to find there was already an inscription. He glanced at it hastily:

> To my beloved grandson, Mark. May he understand the secret of the karst and why it was necessary. Your loving grandpops.

Beneath the message was a finely drawn series of minute symbols:

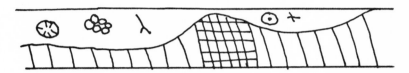

Lyon turned the page, uncapped the pen, wrote his own inscription, and returned the book.

"Thank you. It will make the book more precious to my grandson. I glanced through it at the store; you can't be too careful what you place in the hands of children. It seems to be about some sort of monsters fighting other monsters."

"The Wobblies are the good guys."

"Yes, the Wobblies. And their village is attacked by the . . ."

"Waldoons. They had wings and two heads, as I recall."

"Yes, but not too frightening. I love the Wobblies and I think Mark will too. My only quarrel is that hole the Waldoons come from. You make it seem such a dark, dank place."

"That's probably because I'm a terrible claustrophobic, which is why I prefer hot air ballooning."

"Really, how interesting. I'd like to hear about that. Perhaps on the bus tomorrow?"

"I won't be going with the rest of you. The police want to see me again tomorrow."

"Oh, that's disappointing. Somehow I'd feel safer with you on the bus."

"I'm sure there's nothing to worry about, and I doubt that I could help if there was."

Collins tapped Lyon's photograph on the book. "I've also heard that you sometimes do things of an investigatory nature besides writing your books."

"Once or twice, accidentally."

"There are police in the hallway. Did you know that?"

"Yes, I understand it's purely precautionary and probably designed to calm our fears."

"It could be that the woman who talks about voodoo is right after all."

"I wouldn't have thought you were superstitious, Mr. Collins."

"Demons can take other forms than the strange names she calls them. I'm an accountant by profession, and tend to believe more in the laws of probability and chance. There's a rumor among the passengers that the gun you used this afternoon wasn't yours."

"It belonged to a man sitting behind me."

"Did you know him? Is he here?"

"No, he slipped away. I can hardly recall what he looked like except for his cap and beard."

Collins looked out the window over the darkening city. "A strange set of circumstances."

"You're from Yugoslavia, Mr. Collins."

"Serbia. We used to make a distinction. I didn't realize it still showed after all these years."

"And you aren't a retired army officer."

"You're either very perceptive or make wild guesses."

"You hadn't heard of a two-oh-one file."

"That revealed me. What is it?"

"A service records jacket."

"No. I haven't been in the army. Let's say I was involved in a war of a different sort." He went to the bathroom door. "I know you must be very tired. Good night."

"Good night, Mr. Collins."

Sometime during the night a nightmarish dream of a hundred men with revolvers walking bus aisles jolted Lyon awake. He lay on his side staring across the darkened room. Collins sat hunched in a chair by the window. A flashing neon sign from below intermittently illuminated the lower portion of his face. Lyon watched the sad man in silence for a few moments until waves of sleep again released him.

Police Chief Rocco Herbert didn't hate the state police; he merely liked to avoid them as much as possible. Ordinarily he considered any intrusion into Murphysville matters a violation of his domain, but this morning he had no alternative. The governor had insisted that Bea Wentworth be chauffeured to New York in her official car driven by a state trooper.

He did luxuriate in the width of the rear seat and found he was nearly able to extend his legs their full length. Bea was huddled in the corner staring out the window. "He's all right."

She turned and smiled. "I know. Do you know this is the second time I've seen you in your full dress uniform?"

Rocco reddened. "When was the first?"

"At the Bicentennial parade a couple of years ago." She laughed. "And what in the world are those things on your shoulders?"

Rocco turned a deeper hue of embarrassment. "Stars."

"General's stars?"

"As chief I'm entitled to wear them."

"Rocco Herbert! A twelve-man force and you wear stars?"

"They were Martha's idea. Damn it all, Bea! It won't hurt to impress those jokers in the city."

She gave his shoulder a pat. "I only hope they don't need to be impressed."

The Department of Internal Affairs had provided Lyon with photographs of all men authorized to wear a gold shield in the city of New York. After examining the fiftieth or sixtieth picture, he found they were all beginning to merge into one image, and he wondered if he'd even be able to identify himself. Nevertheless, he kept doggedly at it, looking for the man who had occupied the seat behind him.

They had sequestered him in a small, glass-partitioned cubicle off the main squad room. Captain Nesbitt, McAllister of the FBI, and two men from Internal Affairs were clustered in a small knot near the elevators and occasionally glanced in his direction. He turned the last page of photographs and closed the heavy binder. The man on the bus

34

could have been there, but even a tentative identification was impossible. He left the cubicle and walked toward the officers.

"You buy that cockamamie story of someone slipping him the piece?"

"Hell, no!"

"Does the Pope say mass?"

They laughed.

"We've got to take a position on this," Nesbitt said. "The goddamn mayor is coming down here and the commissioner wants the official line to be lily white."

"Which means we believe he found the gun?"

"You better believe it!" Another officer left the elevator and crossed to them. "There's a mile long Connecticut State car downstairs with a trooper driver and a guy in dress blues that's seven feet tall and must be in charge of every cop in New England."

"We officially believe it," Nesbitt concluded.

They sat in a row along the divan in Nesbitt's office. Rocco seemed uncomfortable in his tight dress uniform, and Bea held her husband's hand tightly.

"We're very proud of your husband, Madam Secretary."

"Please. Call me Bea."

"Of course, and I'm John. In fact," he glanced at his watch, "in an hour the mayor would like to make a presentation with radio and television coverage."

Lyon abruptly went to the window and stood with his back to them. "There will be no coverage as there will be no event to cover."

"Mr. Wentworth, the mayor and police commissioner . . ."

"Am I in custody?"

"Of course not. You can leave at any time. However, we would like you back again if anything further turns up."

"Do you know anything about the man I killed?"

"We haven't had time to complete a full investigation." He picked up a thin file folder. "But there's enough here to tell me he was a real loser."

"May I see it, please?"

John Nesbitt hesitated a moment and then handed over the folder. Lyon stood at the window reading the sparse outline of William

35

Banning Shep's brief life. A room search on East Tenth Street had yielded few possessions except an irate landlady concerned over back rent. His neighbors knew him as a moody, taciturn man who kept to himself; his job history was splotchy, with continued bouts of unemployment. There were several photographs, including a group taken inside the bus, that showed the dead man sprawled in the aisle as Lyon so vividly remembered. He closed the file and gave it back to Nesbitt. "I'm going home now."

Rocco sat in front with the trooper driver while Lyon stared moodily out the rear window. He was unable to shake the sheen of depression that engulfed him. He had tried to view the events with logic, but coherent thought could not dispel his depression.

"You shouldn't have looked at the file."

He didn't answer for a moment. "How's the campaign coming?"

"Lousy. My unworthy opponent has accused me of everything except soliciting votes on my back, and I believe that'll be suggested next week. Did you know that I'm a dupe of the Communist party?"

That penetrated his depression and he smiled. "What kind of dupe are you: Russian, Maoist, Red Guard, or CP U.S.A.?"

"He doesn't know the difference."

"Is he reaching the voters?"

"He talks a lot about what haunts people: taxes, crime, inflation. People hear what they worry about."

"I keep going over it again and again."

"I was afraid of that."

"He keeps coming down the aisle and I'm holding that damn gun in my lap. There must have been another way."

"I've thought about it, and I could never see what else you could have done under the circumstances."

"There are always alternatives."

"Not in this case."

Rocco turned toward them and pointed out the window. They were overtaking a Nutmeg Transportation Company bus. As they passed, the passengers waved out the window. Lyon recognized Hannon, with his arm in a sling, the voodoo lady, and a few others. He gave them a thumbs-up sign as they pulled past the bus and it began to recede in the distance.

He wondered if he'd ever see any of them again. The camaraderie of the cocktail party the night before had been strong, and the promise of a yearly reunion well-intentioned, but might be forgotten as life continued and feelings diminished.

An accident of life had taken a dozen and a half people and put them into extraordinary circumstances. For the present they were riding an emotional high, but it would fade, just as he hoped the face of the man he had killed would eventually go away.

But there had been an additional passenger—the man with the beard who gave him the gun. Why did he leave and disappear?

The shock wave from the explosion was sufficiently powerful to rock the heavy car.

"What in hell was that!" The trooper driver fought the wheel and glared into the rearview mirror.

A plume of black smoke had mushroomed skyward. A second explosion shattered it into long streamers.

"Get back there fast!" Rocco yelled at the driver.

"Yes, sir!" Without further instruction, the driver swerved onto the grass, bumped across the median divider, and swiveled into the far lane. He accelerated toward the burning wreckage.

Bea put her hands to her face. "Good Lord, it's the bus!"

4 The bus straddled the highway with flames lapping from its shattered windows and its interior a smoking mass. The state car made a sweeping skid back across the dividing median and screeched to a stop thirty yards from the inferno. Miraculously other cars had been far enough behind the explosion to remain untouched by fire, but they were now splayed and stalled in odd positions across the road.

Rocco and Lyon slammed from the car and sprinted toward the wreckage. A final scream issued from the bus and then abruptly died.

Rocco had snatched a small fire extinguisher from under the dashboard and held an arm protectively across his face as he fought to work his way toward the door. Intense heat drove him back, and the large chief stood helplessly with the extinguisher dangling uselessly from his hand.

The cause of the explosion seemed to be a 38-ton propylene truck that had pulled from the nearby service area directly into the side of the bus. The single tank had ruptured, and within seconds of the collision the explosion had occurred.

Their driver was speaking frantically into the car's two-way radio, while Bea had discovered a first aid kit in the car trunk.

"Is there anything we can do?" she asked.

Rocco's response went unheard as another explosion rocked the wreckage and nearly knocked them over. He turned toward the gathering crowd and waved his arms. "Get back! Back!"

A lone siren could be heard in the distance as Bea walked away from the bus toward the side of the road.

A strangled groan came from a shallow gully a dozen feet from the edge of the pavement.

She stumbled across the grass and found him where he'd been thrown, face down in the gully. His feet were bare and white in contrast to his blackened back and arms. She stooped and turned him over. He groaned again.

She recoiled back from the contorted face and sightless eyes. What remained of his clothing hung in scorched tatters, and yet, unaccountably, an arm sling was untouched. She ripped the cover from the first aid kit and searched through the meager contents for something useful. What she needed was morphine, but that would have to wait until the ambulances arrived.

The charred caricature of a man groaned again as an arm reached toward her. "Mother, is that you?"

"Yes." She felt his fingers brush against hers and close over her hand.

"It's me. Bobby. Bobby, Mother."

"Only a little while now, Bobby." Her free hand still searched frantically through the first aid kit.

He mumbled something and she bent closer to his mouth to catch the rasping words. A strong wind swept from the north and the words were lost as his hand fell limply from hers.

Bea Wentworth stood slowly. She looked at the thin vial of burn cream clutched in her hand and then down at the body shriveled in the gully. A tear peaked at the corner of her eye and started a slow course down her face, and then her shoulders heaved and she cried in silent sobs.

Vehicles converged on the now smoldering bus: three ambulances, fire equipment, and state police cruisers swiveled in concentric patterns around the wreckage. Ambulance doors slammed open and stretchers were wheeled across the pavement. Firemen ran toward the bus. They ended their dash by joining the others as silent spectators.

A fireman in an asbestos suit and face mask entered the bus. They saw his dim figure through the smoke as he moved awkwardly down the aisle and then back out.

The suited fireman pulled off the hood, shook his head at the others, and then turned to retch in the grass.

Lyon walked to the tanker that had rammed into the bus. The tank had ruptured violently, and flames had moved across the cab and onto the bus. He looked at the present position of the two vehicles, mentally aligned them back to the moment of impact, and backtracked the trajectory of the tanker as it left the service area.

It didn't make sense.

The tanker driver had a clear view of the highway, and yet had to accelerate to the maximum speed his lower range of gears would allow in order to ram the bus at that angle. Unless the driver had a heart attack at the wheel when he was leaving the service area—but in that instance, the tanker would not have run the course it had.

He climbed the tanker's step and peered into the still smoldering cab, the metal hot to his touch. The burned body of the driver lay on the floorboards half under the well and over the accelerator.

He turned from the tanker and walked through the onlookers now being pushed back toward the service area by newly arrived state troopers. The men he wanted to speak to were standing under a high lamp post. They were young, both acne-faced, and wore service station coveralls with their names inscribed over a breast pocket.

"Do you two work at the gas station in the service area?"

They looked at him blankly a moment. "You a cop, huh?"

"You work here?"

"Yeah."

"Did you see it happen?"

"Heard it."

"What about before the explosion?"

"Nothing much. I pumped him fifty gallons of diesel and he left."

"Did he look all right, the driver I mean?"

"Sure. Looked like everybody else, but musta' been crazy as a loon to pull out like that."

"Did he pull directly onto the highway, or did he stop at all?"

"I didn't notice."

"I think he did," the other attendant said. "He stopped by the post

40

up there and talked to a guy for a couple of minutes. I figured it was his bookie."

"Anything else?"

"Hell, we get lotsa cars backed up in here, can't stand gawking at every tanker driver that pulls out."

A state police captain had arrived and was giving directions through a bullhorn. A large wrecker had jackknifed the bus away from the tanker and was attempting to wedge it over onto the median. Traffic had begun to flow slowly along one lane of traffic.

"I hope they have pictures of the relative positions of the two vehicles before they moved them," Lyon said to Rocco who stood next to Captain Norbert of the state police.

"Of course we have pictures," the captain snapped. "This is going to be one hell of a lawsuit."

"Good. You're going to need them for more than lawsuits."

"Wentworth! How in hell did you manage to get here?"

Rocco Herbert glared at his brother-in-law. "Leave him be, Norbie."

"Do we have pictures? Of course we have pictures. We always take pictures at accidents—even bad ones like this."

"I'm afraid it's not an accident, Captain. More like multiple murder."

The Wentworth home, Nutmeg Hill, perched on a promontory overlooking the Connecticut River. Over the years, Lyon had cut a small path with switchbacks into the side of the hill that wound its way through the pine forest studding the side of the mountain down to the river. They walked hand in hand, letting the sun brush lightly against their faces as it cut intermittent swathes through the dense foliage.

At the bottom they stopped near a rock grouping where the river gently lapped. Lyon sat on the ground with his back against a tree trunk, while Bea sat a few feet in front of him on a rock with her bare feet dangling in the water.

The apposition between the serenity of this quiet place on the river and the scene they had witnessed a short time ago numbed them. Bea looked down at her wavering reflection in the water, her rippling image appearing as a skewered tragic mask—a face drawn in the reflection of horror. She had seen people die before. A few years before, within a year of each other, her parents had died. They had died in a quiet room filled with solicitous people and the beep of nearby machinery, their discomfort stilled with painkilling drugs—not unexpectedly in an inescapable oven. She ran her fingers along the contours of her face.

"Is there ever a why? Is it possible that today was just some crazy coincidence?"

"I don't think so."

"The young man in the ditch that I saw die . . . did you know him?"

"His name was Robert Hannon. He was to be a junior at Wesleyan this fall."

"The one who was shot by the hijacker?"

"Yes." He walked to the water's edge and stood near his wife's shoulder. "Those people, all who died this afternoon, had an unusual feeling toward me, as if I were their talisman or protector, and in one woman's case, her Rada. And yet, I somehow have the feeling that I was the instrument of their destruction. If the hijacking had continued until stopped by the police, today might not have happened."

"That's not true. You had nothing to do with the bus fire."

"Last night I held an old woman and promised her she was safe."

"You can't assume guilt like that."

"What did Donne say? 'And therefore never send to know for whom the bell tolls, it tolls for thee.' "

She buried her head in his shoulder so that he would not see her cry. "Stop, stop, stop . . ."

Their wavering images reflected in the river swells merged.

Bea's martini was too large and she talked too quickly and too intensely for her actions to be anything but a nervous attempt to remove the guilt Lyon voiced. Rocco Herbert listened, stared at the ice in his vodka, and occasionally nodded.

"It was an accident, Rocco. The tanker driver had a heart attack. It happens all the time. He pulled onto the highway, blacked out, and his truck went out of control and collided with the bus."

"The medical examiner took a look as soon as we got the body of the driver to the medical center."

"A stroke . . .?"

Rocco shook his head. "If Lyon hadn't alerted us, we might have missed it, considering the condition of the deceased. It was a small-caliber bullet with an entrance wound above the hairline at the back of the head."

"Someone at the service area would have heard the shot."

Rocco shook his head again. "The discharge of a small weapon near the truck stop would have gone unnoticed."

"Damn! Damn! Damn!" Bea went to the bar cart to freshen her drink, and Lyon noticed that her fingers shook.

"Any trace of an explosive device?"

"The bomb squad picked up a small residue of thermite."

"It's becoming as common as ordinary dynamite."

"They reconstruct that it was placed directly under the tank. And now there are seventeen dead."

"Seventeen?"

"Fourteen passengers and the driver, the tanker driver, and the hostess."

"Someone's missing?"

"You! Thank God!" Bea said.

"No, another one of the passengers. I wonder who it is?"

"It'll take a while to make a positive ID here. Let me put in a call to Nesbitt in the city and see what he knows."

As Rocco went to use the phone in the kitchen, Kimberly Ward called from the foyer. "Anybody home?"

"In the study," Bea called back and hiccuped.

Kim came into the room and immediately put her arms around Bea. "The commissioner came to the office and told me about it. Oh, Bea. How horrible."

As the two women talked in low tones, Lyon leaned back in the leather recliner and let the sherry warm between his palms. Gold-orange streaks of sun were visible through the window overlooking the river, and the approaching twilight seemed to accentuate the greenery outside. The drinks must have helped, but the serenity of the house and the presence of their two closest friends seemed to suspend them temporarily in a protective cocoon.

Rocco and Kim were studies in contrast. The bearlike police officer

43

had been a working friend in Korea, a natural arrangement between Ranger and intelligence officer. Their friendship had grown to one of mutual respect and ease in each other's company. He had seen Rocco disarm a man and, on one necessary occasion, beat another into insensibility, just as he had watched him read to a small daughter with a kitten perched on his shoulder.

Several years ago Kim had confronted Bea on a protest march. They had argued violently, still did, and the trim black woman had reluctantly left her revolutionary battlements to become Bea's aide and now Deputy Secretary of the State. If they won the primary and general elections, she would be his wife's congressional aide.

Rocco returned from the kitchen. "One of the passengers left the hotel early this morning."

"Who?"

"They identify him as Major Collins."

"He just walked away?"

"That's what the cop on duty said. They had no reason to detain him."

"We shared a room last night. During our talk he admitted that he lied about his army rank. I wonder if Collins is even his name."

"Nesbitt's men would have taken down ID on all the passengers when they took their statements."

"I wonder if his can be verified?"

"What are you driving at?"

"I have the feeling we ought to look further into Collins."

The door chime hadn't finished its short two-note sequence before the impatient caller began to pound on the door.

"Only fuzz pounds like that," Kim said. "And since we got local fuzz already here, that's state fuzz."

"My brother-in-law," Rocco said. "Come in, Norbie."

Captain Norbert did not enter rooms, he conquered them. In contrast to his earlier appearance at the death scene when he wore knife-creased trousers, tailored jacket, and the wide trooper hat exactly two fingers from the bridge of his nose; he now wore plaid Bermuda shorts, a green sport shirt with a large yellow alligator over the pocket, and a flat madras hat.

"My God!" Rocco said. "Where'd you get that costume?"

"Why in hell aren't you where you're supposed to be, Chief? And when did you move the police station?"

"Last month."

"I passed it three times and thought it was a Reform synagogue."

"That's modern architecture."

"Thank God I don't live in this town. Musta' shot all hell out of the mill rate."

"Federal funds, Norbie. All in knowing how to apply. In fact, I'm thinking of getting a helicopter next."

"A helicopter? In Murphysville?"

Rocco shrugged. "Well, we might have a forest fire sometime. What are you doing in that getup?"

"I was on the golf course with the major when I had a thought."

"One of the biggest crimes in our history and you're out on the golf course?"

"My men had their assignments."

"I know my assignment," Bea said as she mixed a pitcher of martinis. "Good evening, Captain."

Norbert immediately pulled off his cap and made a bow toward Bea. "Madam Secretary."

"Not that. Please not that." She took the martinis in one hand and led Kim by the other to the kitchen.

"I know," Rocco said. "You need us to complete your foursome."

"Hardly. The major and I were at the seventh hole. That's the one with the dogleg to the right."

"I know it," Lyon said. "Had to land my balloon there once. There was a fifteen-mile-an-hour wind from the north, and that's bad for a balloon. When I pulled the ripping panel . . ."

"You two aren't for real!" Rocco exploded. "Golf and balloons after murder?"

"Terrorists, Rocco. That's what I'm trying to tell you. The major and I conjecture that the hijacker Lyon shot was part of a larger group that was going to make political demands at a later time. They never got the chance, and for that they want revenge. That's how we read their motive in going after the bus."

"And didn't the passengers say he mentioned the Freedom Army —whoever they are?"

"Yes, but what sort of terrorists are they?" Lyon asked mildly.

"Who the hell knows these days? Look at the groups we know about: frogs in Canada, Brittany wants out of France, the Moluccans, whoever the hell they are, want something. Croatians want to be cut away—those Italian groups and Irish. Well, you know how they are."

"Since I'm half Irish and half Italian," Rocco said, "how about Panthers or Muslims?"

"Could be."

"Right-wing Republicans," Lyon added.

Norbert vented his anger directly at Lyon. "Don't smart ass me, Wentworth. You know, it's citizens like you who think tragedies are funny that make our jobs more difficult."

"You know, Norbie, you are a horse's ass," Rocco said.

"I expect that from you. Wentworth here would still be in hot water in New York if I hadn't vouched for him."

"What now?"

"We're directing all our energies on the terrorist angle."

"I'd like to know more about the passengers who weren't on the bus."

"You're sitting right here."

"There's another one," Rocco said. "I ran it through NYPD. One didn't take the bus this morning. What else do you have?"

"You know about the pathology report on the driver. We've also interviewed people at the service island. One of the attendants thinks someone was talking to the tanker driver, but no real description. That's all, period. Senseless, which is why we lean toward terrorists."

"What about the passengers that were killed?"

"Of course we'll run checks on all of them to see if anyone had insurance in large amounts, unhappy relatives, or lovers. All that sort of thing to dig for other motives. But they came from all over New England; it will take time."

"I feel that mathematical probability precludes the type of coincidences that happened to that bus," Lyon said.

"A hijacking and murder."

"Unless they were somehow related."

"There could be other explanations."

"Like what?"

"I don't know."

46

"I came over here to get a rundown on the passengers for possible political motives. Well?"

"During the evening we spent together it never came up."

Rocco heaved himself erect and pushed his brother-in-law by the shoulders. "Come on Norbie. If Lyon had anything he'd give it to you."

"Wentworth! Why is it always Wenthworth?" Lyon heard the state police captain say to Rocco as they trudged across the drive to their respective cars.

He found them sitting on the kitchen counter with wide vacant grins and the empty martini pitcher between them. Kim giggled and Bea hiccuped.

"You're both squiffed."

"IT HASN'T BEEN MY MOST FAVORITE DAY, WENT-WORTH," Bea said, hiccuped again, and dropped her hearing aid into the empty martini pitcher.

"Yesterday wasn't a winner for me either." He momentarily considered joining them, but rejected the thought with the knowledge that they had too much of a head start. "Beddy-bye time."

Bea nearly fell from the counter and steadied herself with both hands. "Yes, let us cross over the river and rest under the shade of the trees."

"Stonewall Jackson on his deathbed," Kim said. "How about, 'Show me the trees, Lennie.' "

"Trees?"

"Rabbits, then, something like that."

"Oh, boy." Lyon helped Kim from the counter. He guided her into the living room and let her fall face forward, fully clothed onto the couch. Before he could cover her with a light blanket she had turned on her side and begun to snore lightly.

The phone rang as he returned to the kitchen and he picked it from the wall mounting. "Yes?"

"Lyon Wentworth?"

"Yes."

"I saw it on television news tonight—about the bus. Surprised to hear from me?"

"Who is this?" Bea had her arms around his neck and nibbled at his ear.

47

"You know damn well who it is, Wentworth. And after yesterday and today, you can hardly be surprised that I know who you are. Jesus, a whole bus! You really don't give a damn, do you? I know you had to waste that punk yesterday, but a whole bus."

"Who is this?" Lyon asked again as Bea's hand flipped open the buttons of his shirt.

"The old man wanted me to congratulate you. You took care of both our problems."

"What problem?"

"You know damn well what problem, and you destroyed the merchandise, too. We'll take the usual steps tomorrow." The phone clicked dead.

"An admirer?" she asked and kissed him.

5 As he parked in front of the Murphysville police station,
Lyon decided that possibly Norbie was right. The building
did resemble a Reform synagogue. The similarity wasn't so
much in the lines of the low windows as the mural on the side that
could be construed as a burning bush.

He entered the small lobby with its glass partition and stopped
when he heard the sound of Muzak. Shaking his head, he bent toward
the speech hole. A pert policewoman with shiny cheeks, sitting before a massive group of radio equipment and a computer terminal,
smiled at him. He had the impression of being in a dentist's reception area rather than the cramped police headquarters scrunched
between the village library and the tax assessor's office that he had
been used to.

"Rocco around?"

"Chief Herbert? One moment, sir." She pressed a button on a
console and her low conversation was lost to Lyon. The policewoman
was another addition, and then he remembered that Mary Douglas,
who had fought the ancient telephone switchboard and sometimes-
working radio system for years, had retired last month.

She gave him a smile again and sounded a buzzer that opened a door to the station's interior. "The chief expects you, sir. Second door to the right."

Rocco's brogans had already rutted two lines into the shiny surface of the long mahogany desk. On a credenza to his rear the familiar old percolator still wheezed. Some things didn't change.

Lyon shook his head. "The computer terminal's new and so is the twenty-year-old desk sergeant."

"She's not a sergeant. Like the hardware, huh? You ought to see the pistol range in the basement and the new cruisers."

"But Muzak?"

"That was Martha's idea, but the rest is courtesy of Uncle Sam's LEAA funds with matching state grants. You name it and I've applied for it. Did I tell you about the helicopter?"

"How about a SWAT team?"

"Do you know they tried to give me an armored personnel carrier and some bazookas?"

"For the school crossing guards, no doubt."

"Funny." Rocco slipped a typewritten list across the desk. "Here's the list of deceased passengers."

"What about Collins?"

"Negative. The information he listed was fake. He gave a nonexistent address in Orlando."

"Anything else?"

"Nope. They're still running down all the families of the victims, checking with the insurance companies and all that, but it'll take days."

"So, everyone is looking in Collins' direction?"

"Whose name isn't Collins. The only thing they have to go on is a photograph taken of him after the hijacking incident."

"He could be running from something else."

"I know. A wife, another crime."

"I have the feeling that Collins is tied into all that happened."

"NYPD hasn't been able to turn up any link between any of the passengers and the hijacker. Norbie could be right, the killings could be a terrorist act."

"I had a strange phone call last night. A man said he'd seen the bus

50

fire on the television news. I was supposed to know him. He said he knew I had to take out the hijacker, but why a whole bus?"

"Sounds like a crank call."

"He ended up by saying that I had taken care of both problems and that they'd take the usual steps."

"A nut."

"Maybe."

"What did he sound like?"

"General American dialect with nothing distinctive about his voice."

"Then I wouldn't pay any attention to it."

The telephone on Rocco's desk buzzed melodically. The large chief flicked the receiver to his ear, nodded into it, and hung up. "NYPD has sent up a liaison detective to hold our hands."

"Why here?"

"You got me." He opened the door and admitted a bulky thirtyish man in rumpled clothes. Rocco stuck out his hand with a grip Lyon knew was reserved for occasions of this sort, and he inwardly winced at the pressure he knew would be applied on the New York detective's hand. "Rocco Herbert."

"Sean Hilly." He didn't wince.

"Grab a chair, Hilly. You got ID?"

The detective slouched into a side chair and flipped his wallet across the desk at Rocco. Rocco examined the identification closely, looked up at the detective twice, slowly folded the wallet, and handed it back. "Detective Sergeant Hilly, this is my friend, Lyon Wentworth."

Lyon and Hilly waved at each other.

"I don't understand this liaison bit," Rocco said. "You've got the wrong jurisdiction. The state cops are handling this one. If you want the guy to contact, see Captain Norbert at the barracks."

"Somebody else will cover that. The commissioner is very concerned about this situation, feels that the honor of the city is at stake or some goddamn thing. We want that nothing happens to Mr. Wentworth."

"I'm staying off buses for a few days."

Rocco leaned back in the groaning swivel chair. He folded his arms behind his neck and glared at the other police officer. "We think we're capable of taking care of Lyon."

"I didn't know I had to be taken care of." Lyon had the feeling his remark was lost in the obvious antagonism between the two law officers.

Sean Hilly smiled crookedly and threw a rumpled leg over the chair arm and fumbled for a cigarette from a crushed pack in his shirt pocket. "Let me say that I didn't ask for this assignment. I got night courses at John Jay and don't need time here in the boonies."

Rocco's chair creaked forward as his facial muscles relaxed. "Okay, it's not your fault. They dig up anything in the city?"

"Not that I know of. I was off yesterday and got the call at home to come up here."

"Where do you live in the city, Sergeant?" Lyon asked.

"Me? Live in that cesspool? Hell, I got a nice split out on the Island."

"Since I'm not investigating this case," Rocco said, "what are we supposed to liaison about?"

"Got me. They just want me up here. Told me to keep a low profile and an eye on Wentworth."

"Because most of the witnesses are dead?"

The detective shrugged. "Something like that."

"It might not be a bad idea to keep low for a while, Lyon."

"That's what our people thought," Hilly said as he located a battered cigarette lighter, which he tried to work, to no avail.

"Not necessarily so," Lyon said. "We don't know the motive behind the destruction of the bus. One thing I do know is that I do not possess any information that would justify anyone making an attempt on my life."

Sergeant Hilly's face curved into a smile. "Okay, Wentworth. You're on home turf and outa' our jurisdiction. Come on, tell me. It was your gun that you used to blow away the bastard, wasn't it?"

"No."

"You saw who slipped it to you?"

"He was behind me."

"You'd recognize him?"

"I don't think so."

"Maybe he doesn't know that."

"We're not even sure if there is a connection between the man who gave me the gun and all else that happened."

"Doesn't hurt to be safe," Rocco said. "Why don't you and Bea take a vacation? To Bermuda? In fact, don't tell anyone where you're going."

"Bea's in the midst of a primary fight—impossible."

"That's what I was afraid of. Come on, let's get some lunch."

Sarge's Bar was squeezed between two clapboard three-family homes in a predominantly residential area. The local zoning board defended this nonconformity by using as their defense that when Sarge Renfroe applied for a permit, they couldn't understand what he was saying. Since the board met at eight in the evening, and Sarge was rarely decipherable after seven, this could very well be true.

Rocco parked and turned to Hilly in the rear seat. "Not much to look at, but he serves a generous roast beef sandwich at a good price."

Hilly looked at the bar's facade with an arched eyebrow. "You country cops got it made. They don't like us going into places like this unless we're working vice."

"Huh?" Rocco turned toward the front of the building. His mouth gaped open as he vaulted from the car to examine the large banner draped across the front of the building. "Oh, my God!"

GRAND OPENING
SARGE'S TOPLESS FROLICS

Inside, they saw that the liquor bottles and streaked mirror had been removed from behind the bar to make room for a small runway. Speakers on either side blared loud disco while a topless dancer in bikini panties gyrated awkwardly. The booths and bar stools had been ripped out and piled in the backyard and were replaced by a mass of small tables and straight chairs. The former regulars sat sullenly in a far corner clutching their draft beers.

"Renfroe!" Rocco's voice cut over the loud music. Sarge, who had been leaning against the ancient cash register admiring the dancer, jerked erect and turned to wave a damp bar cloth at Rocco. "Come over here, Renfroe."

"I appreciate you guys showing me the high spots of Murphysville," Hilly said, "but I can get this stuff better in Times Square."

Lyon thought of Wobblies and wondered if they were sitting in the police cruiser outside with disapproving glares. "This is a new addition," he finally managed to say without laughing aloud.

Rocco and Sarge were now by the door where Rocco's finger shook under the cowering retired noncom's nose.

"You got no right!" Sarge's voice rose over the music.

"Girl on the stage can't dance," Hilly said, "but she's got a good bod."

"That's Katty Hemphill," Lyon replied. "She looks better since her acne went away."

"Who's looking at her face? Or is she jailbait?"

"She was a high school senior last year so she must be over eighteen." Lyon left the table to walk toward the men arguing by the door. He glanced at Katty Hemphill and decided she'd look a lot better if she learned to dance without chewing gum. Rocco was reddening as his anger became more obvious. It was time to put a stop to things. "Did you tell Sarge about the liquor laws?"

"What laws?"

"About serving alcoholic beverages within the city limits under these circumstances."

"The chief's got no right to put me out of business. You know what I can clear topless?"

"You're right, Sarge," Lyon replied. "And all you have to do to keep him out of your hair is to serve near beer and nonalcoholic wine. Then you're home free."

"No kidding?"

"That's what the better dirty places in New York do."

"Right, Chief?" He turned to Rocco beseechingly.

Rocco glanced sideways at Lyon as the anger drained from his face. "That's about it, First. Take out the booze and you can have orgies in here."

"Great, man. Great." Sarge turned, took two steps before spinning back toward them. "Take out the booze? You're crazy!"

"It's sort of up to you, Sarge. Booze or boobs, so to speak."

"That right?" He looked quizzically from Rocco to Lyon.

"Absolutely," Lyon said.

Sarge Renfroe considered his alternatives for three seconds before turning back toward the bar. "Katty Hemphill! Get the hell off there and get some clothes on!"

54

Sean Hilly nearly choked on a large mug of beer as they sat down. "You're all right, Wentworth. All right. I hope to God you don't get knocked off."

The Secretary of the State for Connecticut sat behind her desk before blue drapes and deep carpeting and despised herself for the massive headache that consumed her.

Kimberly Ward, deputy to the Secretary, clutched a clipboard before her as she sat heavily on the long couch. "You want to go over this list or just call it a day?"

"At nine in the morning?"

"Well, there is one minor little item on today's agenda."

"Nothing requiring a great deal of effort, I hope."

"The document is called the constitution of the state, and it seems to require that you officially put the legislature in recess today."

Bea groaned. The constitution stipulated the length of the legislative session, and midnight today was the mandatory recess time. She remembered two years ago when the state income tax bill was under debate and they'd forced her to stop the clock at five minutes to the witching hour. The clock had remained stopped for eight hours. "How's the calendar look?"

"They moved along fine yesterday, but you know how it is at the end of the session."

"Maybe they'll voice vote."

Kim raised an eyebrow. "In an election year? I could get my more militant friends to make a bomb threat."

Bea put her head in her hands. "Promises, promises. Anything else on your doomsday board?"

"Dottie took a call first thing this morning." She glanced at the board. "A Mr. Raven Marsh has an appointment to see you. He says he's a free-lance writer."

"Not today."

"Too late. He's on his way. You can't cancel appointments with news writers and win elections."

"What paper is he with?"

"A magazine writer. Then there's the delegation from Miss Porter's school at eleven, and a speech before the University Club at noon."

"Will my opponent be there?"

"You know it."

"This afternoon we can sleep it off."

"At two the new interns from Trinity, a news conference at six. You had better have a short dinner and get back, in case the legislature manages to break early."

Bea took the clipboard from Kim and contemplated the day's activities. They were a fine testimonial for abstinence. The intercom rang and she answered with a "Yes, Dottie?"

"A Mr. Raven Marsh is here to see you."

"Show him in."

The day had begun.

6 Intermittent bursts of jagged flame ejaculated into the fog. Lyon steered his pickup off the highway onto a grassy slope and slowed to a stop. He bent over the steering wheel and craned his neck to look up at the large round shapes spotted across the field that were beginning to rise through the mist.

"You'll have to admit they are beautiful."

Bea yawned. "Nothing is beautiful at six in the morning."

"As soon as the sun's well up, this fog will burn off. The weather report says a three-to-four-mile-an-hour wind. It's going to be perfect launch weather."

Bea yawned again and covered her mouth with her hand. "Excuse me if I continually fail to get excited over hot air balloons."

He put the truck in gear and began to move slowly across the field, threading his way around campers, station wagons, and other pick-ups, all next to balloons in varying stages of inflation. A man stepped directly in their path and raised both hands. Lyon braked and rolled down the window. "Morning, Max. Looks like a better turnout than last year's meet."

Maximus Popov, bearded, with bandy legs and casklike torso now partially covered by a bright red down vest, walked toward the truck and leaned in the window. "That you, Wentworth?"

" 'Tis, professor. Where do you want me?"

"Over in the north corner, right behind the rig with the pirate on the side. I'll be over to see you a little later." He gave Lyon a mock salute and turned to face another vehicle.

Moving at only a few miles an hour they wove their way past a dozen vehicles and around outstretched balloon envelopes in different stages of inflation. They parked at the far side of a black balloon with a thirty-foot Jolly Roger on its side. In movements rehearsed in long practice, they both left the truck and lowered the tailgate. Lyon rolled the Wobbly III onto the grass.

They worked silently and efficiently, unrolling the long envelope on the still damp meadow grass and then positioning the basket on the ring secured below the balloon bag. Lyon knelt next to the portable air compressor and pulled the start rope three times before the small engine coughed into life and began to pump air into the bag. As cool air began to fill the envelope, it billowed out on the ground, jouncing slightly from the surface.

Hooking the propane burner to a tank, Lyon held the unit across his body, beckoned to Bea who stepped aside, and ignited the device.

A three-foot spear of flame jutted through the early light. He made adjustments to the feed while Bea held the balloon aperture apart.

"Okay?"

"As we'll ever be."

As flame continued to shoot into the envelope, it began to heat the cool air. The balloon began to fill and bob from the surface until within minutes it was in an upright position. As soon as it was fully erect and steady, he attached the burner to the fixture above his head in the gondola basket. From this juncture, only occasional bursts from the burner were needed to keep the balloon in gravitational balance.

Popov had moved across the field toward them and now stood back from the balloon looking up at the filled bag. "That's the damnedest thing. That face on the balloon. One of your characters?"

"A Wobbly."

"Mean looking bastard."

"What's on the agenda first?"

58

"That's what I want to talk to you about. As soon as everyone's in the air, I'd like to organize a hare and hound."

"And you want me to be the hare?"

"You have as many hours in as anyone. Mind?"

"No, glad to. Tell me when you want me to leave." Lyon turned to make his preflight checks on the balloon and the few instruments mounted in the basket. The sun began to glow a dull red over the horizon; the early fog had somewhat dissipated, although long tendrils still hung over the field and a ground mist swirled at knee height.

Kim was entranced. Her attention was so closely riveted to the man by her side that she missed the turnoff and had to stop and back up to the roped spectator parking area. "How do you know so much about Africa?"

"I spent some time in Kenya with Leakey. Fascinating man, we'll have to talk about him sometime. We there?"

"That we are. Now, come on. We have to find the Wentworth balloon before it takes off."

"Right. Well, anyway, my favorite tribe is the Watusi. Magnificent people, the men all average over six feet in height, and they have some fascinating tribal customs. You know, it's still practically the middle of the night, an excellent time for a frontal assault or hunting, but otherwise all good men and women should be abed."

"Frontal assaults you may have covered, but this is obviously your first hot air balloon meet."

"Matter of fact, it is. I covered Forbes when he attempted a transatlantic crossing, but of course that was a fixed gas vehicle." He pulled a silver flask from his jacket. "Indulge?"

"Hardly ever before eight in the morning."

"A nip before eight is still drinking after dinner."

"We'll miss the inflating."

"Not a chance." Raven Marsh unwound from the small car and tilted back his head to take a swig from the flask. He joined Kim. They stepped over the rope separating the parking area from the launch sites. "Good crowd for so early in the morning."

"There's less wind this time of day and the air heats better."

The loud *whoosh* immediately to his side made Raven jump and nearly fall as he gripped Kim's arm. "My God! What's that?"

"A propane burner. They're used to heat the air."

"Christ! I thought we were under rocket attack."

Kim led Raven through the labyrinth of inflated balloons to where the Wobbly III bobbed at its moorings. Bea waved as they approached, while Lyon was oblivious to them as he continued his preflight checks.

"GLAD YOU COULD MAKE IT, RAVEN. The one in the basket is my husband, Lyon. LYON, MEET RAVEN."

"Huh?" Lyon turned toward them, his mind still filled with calculations. "Hi."

"RAVEN'S DOING THE STORY."

"What story?" Lyon automatically plucked his wife's ear and adjusted the hearing aid.

"You're a fascinating couple, Mr. Wentworth. Your career, your wife's political position, the hijacking incident, and now this. Great! Really great. Hot air ballooning will be the added color we need."

Lyon turned to busy himself with the mooring line. "I don't care to discuss the hijacking. Any coverage of Bea's political race will be appreciated, but I will not talk about the shooting on the bus."

"I wouldn't dream of infringing upon your privacy without your permission."

Mollified, Lyon smiled and reached for Raven's hand. "I'll keep you to that. Glad to meet you."

"What magazine will publish the story?" Bea asked.

*"Playboy."*

"What?" Kim looked incredulous as she turned toward the writer. "You're kidding?"

Raven put his arm around her and smiled. "Hey, sweets, it's not all naked flesh, you know. They publish some of the major writers, and they pay the best."

Several nearby propane burners ignited simultaneously and again Raven Marsh jumped. Over a dozen balloons were now in nearly inflated condition and still others were being off-loaded from trucks and trailers. Several were hovering in the sky with their mooring lines still tethered to car bumpers. It seemed to be a scene of massive animals awakening and unlimbering as they left hibernation for an onslaught against the cloud gods. "Reminds me of WW Two. The Big

Eight in the U.K. Dawn. Engines revving. A toss of the scarf over the shoulder as we bid farewell."

Lyon looked perplexed for only a moment. "Big Eight in the U.K.? You don't look old enough to have served in England with the Eighth Air Force in World War Two."

"Vicariously, Wentworth. Vicariously. I go to a lot of movies."

Lyon looked at the man standing by his gondola. He seemed to be about thirty-five, of average height and weight, dressed in corduroy slacks and matching jacket with leather patches on the elbows. The smile seemed ingenuous, and a small breeze ruffled the reddish hair causing a forelock to spread across his brow.

Kim tapped the writer on the shoulder. "Ah, Raven, about the article. Exactly what sort of photographs do you plan to use?"

"Well, I thought we'd get a shot of Bea stretched out on that long couch in her office. Au naturel, of course. But because of her prestigious position, I shall let her clutch a copy of the state constitution in an appropriate place."

"And you will go up in the balloon—hanging by your feet."

Raven laughed. "You're jealous, sweets. You want to be the centerfold. I can see the caption—Black Beauty with angry visage."

"How about dropping dead?"

"Come on, you should know me better than that. I'll take some shots of everyday things. But this balloon business is a natural. I ought to get some great pictures. Where's my camera?"

"You left it on the back seat of the car."

"Be right back."

They watched him hurry toward the spectator parking lot, making wide detours around balloons with active burners.

"Is he for real?" Bea asked.

"He's been everywhere," Kim replied. "And according to him, done everything."

"How long is he going to be with us?"

"He didn't exactly say. Only that he thought we'd be good material for a story and the magazine thought so also."

"Particularly after the hijacking."

Max Popov lumbered toward them as the last remnants of the morning fog burned off the meadow. On the highway they could see

61

a steady stream of spectator cars pulling into the lot. More balloons were in the air, some ascending a hundred feet to the farthest extent of their mooring lines and then descending. Lyon stood in his basket ready for flight and awaited Popov with anticipation.

"Come over to my camper, Wentworth. Let's plan this here shindig."

Lyon glanced up at the balloon to make sure it had enough stability to remain upright.

"I know," Bea said. "We'll look after your balloon toy until you get back."

Lyon and Popov walked toward the small trailer at the far corner of the field. "Great day for a meet, great day," Popov said with glee. They entered the trailer where a youngish woman wearing tight jeans, with blond hair cascading down her back, was petulantly looking at a coffeepot on the two-burner stove. She waved at Lyon as the two men bent over a map laid out on the Formica-topped table.

"How's the wind and direction?" Lyon asked.

"Four miles from the southeast. That'll give you a clear shot at the ridges to the north, or up the valley. Watch out for Hawkins Pond. I don't feel like wading in after people."

"What about power lines?" The unspoken fear between the two men was the fatal danger to their cumbersome vehicles if they approached a high tension line at low altitude.

"There's a heavy line to the west. You should be well away of it unless there's a radical change of wind."

"Good. I'll go up to five hundred, stop, then to a thousand. One rapid descent and then a fast ascent."

"Sounds good. You have someone to chase for you?"

"My wife will follow me."

"Good flight. I'll give you a four-minute start."

"You're on."

Popov folded the map and handed it to Lyon. "Good luck."

Lyon took the map and glanced down at the legend on its face and read it aloud, "Do not use for navigational purposes after 1970?" He looked up at Popov.

"Don't worry. I know the area." He thumped Lyon's shoulder. "Take off as soon as you can."

"Right." He walked back to the Wobbly III, which bobbed unattended and had begun to cant to the side. He climbed into the basket and gave the propane a short burn, which righted the envelope. Two balloons away he saw Bea and Kim shaking hands with a group of spectators. She turned in alarm when she heard the sound of the burn.

He would have been annoyed if he weren't so pleased in having Popov select him as the hare. In the several years he had come to the annual New England Balloon Meet, he had never received the honor and now felt that the small ballooning community had finally admitted him into their inner ranks.

He glanced up through the balloon aperture into the bag's interior. The red line running from the basket to the ripping panel was in place and working. In the event of an emergency descent, the panel could be pulled, which tore away a segment of the bag and allowed large gulps of hot air to escape into the atmosphere. It provided for a very rapid descent. He reached over his head and flipped the level of the propane burner, and a spurt of flame spewed into the bag, increasing the interior temperature of the balloon and causing it to bob slightly from the ground.

He tapped the face of the three instruments in the basket and then nodded toward Bea. She untied the mooring line from the bumper of the pickup and he coiled it neatly in the gondola.

With a wave, he gave another burn and the balloon shot upward.

He watched the altimeter closely until it approached 500 feet, and tried to judge his rate of ascent in order to reach level flight as near that altitude as possible. This, like all his subsequent movements, would be imitated by the following hound balloons.

Bea was directly below him, walking to their truck, while to her right Raven was pointing a camera with a zoom lens in his direction. Far to the left a lone bearded figure stood looking upward. There was a familiarity to the man's stance and general configuration, and Lyon had immediate recall of the day in the tunnel as the squad car moved slowly past a group of police. A man in a beard looked directly at him and then turned away. He was probably imagining things, and there would be many bearded men at the meet, including Max Popov.

He took the craft higher, allowed it to stabilize at a thousand feet, and begin to drift north. Bright sun filled the basket as day broke across the side of the balloon. His shadow fell on the fields below in a wide circle, and the silent drift and sensation of free flight filled him with a buoyancy and clarity that had eluded him for days. He gripped the guy wires of two corners of the basket and felt cleansed and whole again.

The hounds began to rise from the ground in their attempt to duplicate Lyon's moves. He waited until they reached his altitude before executing the most dramatic maneuver of the flight.

The careful man glanced from the hovering balloon, with the large Wobbly on its side, down to his watch. He watched with dispassion as the sweep second hand jerked slowly around the dial. It would only be a few more minutes before it began, and then the circle would be complete, the last loose end excised. It was perhaps unfair that Wentworth had an inadvertent choice of roommates that night, but then again, perhaps life was unfair. He looked up at the sky and waited.

Opening the panel at the crown of the balloon, Lyon allowed large gusts of hot air to escape from the envelope. The balloon began an immediate descent. Watching the altimeter and the interior of the balloon, he kept the panel open as long as he dared before slowly closing it. He gave the propane a shot and allowed the balloon to drop within a few feet of the ground. A five-mile-an-hour wind pushed him across an open field toward a distant tree line.

As he approached the trees, he decided it would be best not to get too close as the maneuver might be difficult for some of the more novice ballooners. He increased the burn and the balloon rose swiftly and cleared the trees with fifty yards to spare.

He glanced up at the hounds in the sky attempting to duplicate his maneuvers. It was awesome to see the air filled with a dozen behemoths.

Looking back toward his own forward course, he saw that he was again at treetop level and quickly traversing another field and headed directly toward the pylon of a high tension line.

It wasn't supposed to be there, but it was. The naked rake of earth underneath the lines indicated the newness of its construction.

Unable to change horizontal direction, the balloon moved relentlessly toward the power lines. Lyon knew that pulling the ripping panel would not enable him to pass under the lines, nor could he land in time. Instinctively he pulled down on the propane lever.

The pilot did not light the burner and he pulled the lever again and again without results.

The tanks were empty. Although he always carried enough propane for double the length of any planned flight, inexplicably the tanks were now without fuel.

The lines were only a few feet away from the leading edge of the balloon. He knew of an accident in Georgia a few years ago where the balloonist had died under almost identical circumstances.

Lyon turned from the approaching lines, nearly touching the balloon, and dove over the side of the basket.

7 Willie Shep stood at the end of the long bus with a laugh that began at some distant place and increased in volume as it echoed forward. He began to move down the aisle as a crooked smile cleaved his face. Lyon fired the Magnum and watched the bullet pass harmlessly through the hijacker's body. As his attacker came closer, the other passengers stood and turned with pointed index fingers aimed at Lyon. He recoiled in horror at their dead faces and fired the gun again and again as the laughter increased and was mimicked by the others.

His eyes opened. His breath came in short gasps and he felt pain surrounding his rib cage. As his orientation returned, he saw them bent over the bed: Bea to his side and the bearded man at the foot. He tried to cry out, and again felt the pain.

"He's awake."

"I'll never forgive myself for this," Popov said.

"I'm sure it wasn't your fault."

The room stabilized for Lyon as he tentatively moved his limbs, found them operable, and assessed his injuries as a massive headache with pain girdling his rib cage. "Those lines weren't supposed to be there and the propane ran out. Where am I?"

"The hospital," Bea said. "With cracked ribs and a concussion. They say you can leave after a few days' observation."

"My God, I'm sorry, old man. I really didn't know they were there. They weren't last year."

"The propane tanks had been tapped."

"There must have been a malfunction when they were filled."

"Anyone else hurt?"

"No. They all had time to avoid the lines after they saw what happened to you. Thank God you had presence of mind to leap from the basket instead of trying to ride it down."

"How's the Wobbly III?"

Popov looked embarrassed. "Well, it's still wrapped around the power lines. They caught your balloon between the basket and the envelope, the gondola flipped over the lines in a complete circle. Never saw that happen before."

"Like the Georgia case."

"I guess it is. The electric company people tell me they can cut it down in a day or two, but I'm afraid it's been totaled."

"An old map, lines that weren't supposed to be there, and malfunctioning tanks. That's quite a combination."

"I hope you'll accept my apology for any part I inadvertently played in the accident?" Lyon didn't answer. "If there's anything I can do?" Popov said to Bea. "I'll see about salvage on the balloon and truck what I can to your place."

"Thanks."

"Well, okay, then." He gave a wave and hurriedly exited.

"You don't blame Max?"

"Where's Kim?"

"In the waiting room with Raven. She's torn between worrying about you and some story about an African tribe that's all eight feet tall or something. Raven says he's got a great shot of the accident, but that you didn't have to go to all that trouble on his behalf."

Lyon groaned. "Not on his behalf. I think you had better get Rocco for me."

"You don't think it was an accident?"

"No."

She pulled a chair to the side of the bed and sat as near to him as she could. "I had the binoculars up when it happened and I saw you go over the side of the basket. I thought—well, you can guess what I thought. You know, Wentworth, I wouldn't be at all unhappy if you

67

gave up your hobby for something safe like sky diving or deep sea exploration."

"A balloon is one of the safest vehicles known to man under proper conditions."

"You're no proof of that."

"An out-of-date map, new power lines, no propane. . . . I can't follow the lines of coincidence that far."

"That's pretty subtle and sophisticated sabotage."

Lyon considered the calculations required to have his balloon, under exact wind conditions, at that place and that height when the propane ran out. "Very sophisticated, or else done by someone who was completely unfamiliar with the operation of a hot air balloon. Someone who would not realize that the loss of propane under ordinary circumstances would not mean disaster. It could be very unsophisticated." But sabotage he was certain it was. "I wonder about Popov. He was the one who selected me to be the hare."

"I can't believe that of Max."

"He wears a beard."

"A good many men do nowadays, and beards can be taken off easily."

"He worked on your last campaign, didn't he?"

"Two years ago he handled three towns for me and did a pretty good job. We carried them by a wide majority."

"I only know him through ballooning. What else do you know about him?"

"His parents were Russian emigrés who lived in Paris a good many years. That's where he was born. They went to England during World War Two, and Max came over here when he was eighteen or twenty. Finished his graduate work and now teaches economics at Middleburg College. The blond with him is a permanent house guest. Max balloons, and likes my politics."

"I like your politics, too." They held hands as his eyes closed.

Bea leaned over to kiss him on the forehead, pulled the blanket over his shoulders, and quietly left the room.

68

When he awoke again the day was waning, and the last light cast diffused patterns through the venetian blinds. His body tensed as the door handle turned. It opened slowly to admit a tall, shadowy figure that approached the bed and laid something on the nightstand.

"Rocco?"

"No, Mr. Wentworth. I'm Dr. Warren. May I talk to you a moment?"

"Of course."

The overhead light flickered on to reveal a man carrying a clipboard who sat in the chair next to the bed. He wore a gray herringbone tweed sport jacket with strange green slacks that drew attention from an extremely elongated face dominated by large, lined pouches under the eyes. He seemed to Lyon to be a very sad man.

"The emergency room attending physician asked that I stop in to chat with you."

"I can go home?"

"That's not exactly my province. They were concerned downstairs over certain things you said, certain incoherent things you mumbled."

"I'm afraid that I draw a blank on anything that happened after I hit the ground."

Dr. Warren glanced at his clipboard. " 'He's going to kill me, I know he is going to kill me.' " He looked sadly at Lyon. "I wonder if you could be more explicit than that?"

"I don't know who 'he' is."

"Someone you don't know is trying to kill you?"

"Exactly."

"Do you ever see this individual?"

"I thought I saw him on the ground, and of course he was in the tunnel. At least I think that's the one. The same person who gave me the gun and told me to kill Willie Shep."

"He tells you to kill people." It was a statement, and the doctor wrote a long, meticulous note on his board. "Does he often do that?"

"Only that once."

"Do you hear other voices, Mr. Wentworth?"

"Well, yes. Now that you mention it."

"Do these voices belong to anyone in particular?"

"Usually the Wobblies."

69

"Members of the old IWW?"

"Of course not. The Wobbly monsters. They often walk with me, and come to see me in my study. Ig usually sits on the mantle and Scratch always takes the leather chair. He's a fiend for comfort."

"And you actually see these . . . Wobblies?"

"Oh, yes."

"What do they look like?"

"They're both so alike that it's difficult to tell them apart until they speak. Then it's quite obvious. They are six feet tall, furry, with red eyes and long red tongues that usually loll out the sides of their mouths. Their snouts are long, like their tails, and they look quite fierce until you get to know them."

"I see. And they tell you to do things?"

"Constantly."

"Bad things?"

"Never. They are actually quite benign."

"Except when they give you guns and tell you to kill people?"

"I beg your pardon."

"These . . . these monsters tell you to kill."

"I'm a little confused, doctor."

"Yes, I can understand that. Do you know what day it is?"

"Tuesday? No, yesterday was Wednesday. No. The balloon meets are always held on Saturday morning."

"You're not certain?"

"I do lose track occasionally, but it must be Saturday."

"I see." He wrote another copious note. "These Wobblies talk to you often and for long lengths of time?"

"When I'm alone and working."

"It must be difficult for you to function under those circumstances?"

"On the contrary. I couldn't do it without them."

"Uh huh. And now someone is trying to kill you?"

"I believe so."

"And of course the Wobblies will tell you to kill him first?"

"Absolutely not!" Lyon winced as he sat up. "I think you are the confused one, doctor."

"Your monsters told you that?"

"They didn't have to." Lyon laughed as he realized the significance of the doctor with the long face. "Oh, my God! You're a psychiatrist."

"Uh huh." Another long note.

"An inappropriate response?"

"That sometimes happens. These things do not overcome us overnight, Mr. Wentworth. It often takes years for such symptoms to manifest themselves. And consequently, it will take time for us to remove them and make you well again."

"BEATRICE!"

Dr. Warren jumped at his yell, and reached for the hypodermic he had placed on a towel on the night table. "I have something here that will relax you." He held up the syringe and depressed the plunger to force a drop from the tip.

"No, thank you."

"You will feel much better," the doctor said as he advanced toward the bed.

"No!" Lyon swiveled painfully off the bed in the opposite direction and retreated into a corner. "It's not convenient for me right now. BEATRICE!"

"Please, Mr. Wentworth. We must have your cooperation."

The door burst open as Rocco and Bea rushed in. Rocco assessed the situation, saw the man with the hypodermic needle stalking Lyon in the corner, and drew his service revolver.

"Drop it!"

Dr. Warren turned to stare into the muzzle of a .38. "What?"

"You heard me, drop it." Rocco thumbed the hammer of the revolver back and the click seemed to reverberate throughout the room. The hypodermic clattered to the floor as Dr. Warren backed into the other corner. "Take the position," Rocco thundered.

"What?"

"You heard me. Turn toward the wall, feet out, palms against the wall. Fast!"

Rocco had frisked the psychiatrist, cuffed his hands behind his back, and was preparing for interrogation when the doctor's bloodcurdling cry for help brought three attendants rushing to the room.

"Under Connecticut General Statutes any licensed physician can commit for a period of thirty days any individual who is deemed to . . ."

"Please, Bea. No more. I hurt." Lyon, in the front seat of the Murphysville cruiser, held his sides as he fought to retain his laughter.

"I feel like a damned fool." Rocco hunched over the wheel. "I might have shot the long drink of water."

"Who was he going to certify?"

"All of us, I think," Bea answered. "He didn't have much sense of humor. I still think you should have stayed for a few days of observation."

"I was afraid they'd pad my room while I slept." The codeine they'd given him had driven away most of the headache, but his ribs still ached. He looked down at his torn shirt and blotched pants and decided he looked exactly like what he was—a man who had recently jumped from a hot air balloon.

A smile crinkled the edge of Rocco's mouth. "Okay, it was kind of funny, but what did you want me down here for anyway? Or was this a set-up joke on Rocco?"

Lyon explained the accident. Rocco nodded as he drove, occasionally asking questions, until he had all the details. "Why would anyone want to kill you?"

"Why a whole bus?"

"The state is still working on the terrorist theory."

"Any further word?"

"Negative, and that bothers them. It's usual in cases such as this that the group make contact with a newspaper or radio station to take credit for the act."

"He, she, or they still wanted a lot of people dead."

"Major Collins?"

"Or the missing man who gave me the gun. We've got to find him."

"Who?"

"Both of them."

Martha Herbert, in a long housecoat and her hair wound around fat purple curlers, stood at the front door and pursed her lips as she viewed the entourage on her stoop. She stood aside and let Rocco, Kim, Raven, and Bea enter while Lyon followed last.

"House guests, hon," Rocco said as he leaned over to kiss his diminutive five-foot wife.

"All of them?" she asked in a small voice as her husband made introductions and led them all toward the basement recreation room.

Raven looked at Martha Herbert's short figure swaddled in the voluminous housecoat, and then at the gargantuan Rocco. He looked again, and then leaned over to whisper in Kim's ear.

Kim laughed.

Lyon had always wondered what men whispered into women's ears at parties and cocktail lounges. Perfectly normal-appearing men of routine senses of humor must have some secret reserve of particularly funny things that they hoarded for those occasions. He must ask Bea if she'd ever been whispered at.

The Herberts' daughter, Remley, was in the rec room on the couch with her feet straight up the wall and a phone stuck in her ear. Rocco sent her upstairs for coffee while he pulled the convertible out to its double-bed length.

"Lyon and Bea can stay here tonight. There's no access through the basement except from the upstairs."

"I once saw you sleep through an artillery barrage."

"Martha hears the cat cross the floor, and her punch in my ribs brings me around fast."

"We'd be all right at Nutmeg Hill."

"Maybe and maybe not. I'd like a day to get my equipment set up out there."

"Equipment?"

"I got some great electronic surveillance stuff. Infrared sniper-scopes from the army, that sort of stuff. Turns night into day."

"Matching grants," Lyon and Bea said together.

When Remley served coffee, Raven produced his silver flask and toured the room with a flourishing lace to everyone's cup. Martha and Rocco Herbert refused, Martha with a near indignant toss of her head, Rocco with a wistful nod. When he was finished, Raven stood by the empty fireplace in a stance of anticipation. "Well, when do we begin the investigation? Did I ever tell you about the time I did a story on New Scotland Yard? Fascinating place, and there was one inspector who gave me . . ."

Kim crossed quickly to the writer and grasped him by the elbow.

"If he gets started, we'll be here until dawn listening to his story. Good night, folks." She steered Raven upstairs, his exuberant chatter still audible as they walked through the house.

"No windows near the couch," Lyon mumbled after the others had left.

"What does that mean?" Bea asked as she helped him remove his shirt and pants.

"No lines of fire. We're safe. We can sleep." He sank onto the sofa bed and seemed to fold back against the pillow. "I'll start checking tomorrow."

Bea lifted his feet and pulled the covers over him. "You're in no condition to do anything tomorrow."

"Got to, got to." His voice seemed to fade.

"What will you do first?"

"Check out the hijacker. Have to know if we're dealing with terrorists or what."

She shucked off her clothes down to panties and bra and slid under the sheets next to him. "Lyon."

"Be ready in a minute. Little nap first."

She laughed. "I only wanted you to know how glad I am that you're all right."

"Uh huh."

"Lyon, the balloon. I know it's totally destroyed, but did we have any insurance on it?"

"Cost too much. Remember when the agent came by the house last year?"

"And the balloon cost six thousand."

"Plus accessories."

She heard him begin to snore, and she lay next to her husband and was a little ashamed that she thought about the six thousand dollars.

The Datsun accelerated as she pulled off the entrance ramp and into the fast lane of the interstate highway. It was 140 miles to New York City, and she'd be in midtown in three hours. She'd left a note for Lyon that said she'd gone to the city to shop—and that was only half a lie.

She'd awakened that morning early, instantly alert, and had begun to plan her day, outlining the speech she was to give in Marston that

74

night.Then all political thoughts had vanished, and all she could think of was yesterday at the balloon meet.

Again she saw herself looking through binoculars at the Wobbly III as it inexorably moved toward the high tension lines . . . and then watching him dive from the gondola and fall to the ground. She had sunk to her knees on the grass with her head bent forward, her body forming an S curve of profound grief. She had stumbled toward the field where he lay sprawled across the grass, and then he had moved and groaned.

She wondered if he really knew the extent that she loved him. She tried to express it physically, and yet when she spoke it aloud, it often seemed to come out as a humorous aside rather than an endearment.

Bea knew she was a competitive and often abrasive person. Her battles with life and those things she considered unjust often seemed to consume her, and Lyon so often supplied the relief and tenderness she so desperately needed. She was not whole without him.

8 Bea Wentworth sat on an orange crate holding a Styrofoam cup of tepid coffee between both hands in the back room of Miller's Supermarket on West Fourteenth Street. She wore a rose linen pantsuit with a simple white blouse and very practical shoes. Although she cocked her head attentively, and the small hearing device in her right ear was turned up, she still found it difficult to follow the quixotic train of thought of the assistant manager, Jimmy O'Halloran, as he stood by a wide sink lopping lettuce with a long knife.

"Like I told the cops. He was a real fuc . . . goof-off. I got my break early today. How about a shot at the White Rose?"

"How long did Mr. Shep work here?"

"Mister . . . Jesus . . . nobody called that creep 'mister.' You're not bad, baby. I mean, you're like well preserved, know what I mean? Willie was a loser, you know."

She wondered if being well preserved were a compliment. All things considered, she thought it probably was. She tried again. "He worked here how long?"

"The cops were all over my ass. Dragged me out of bed. Christ, youda' thought . . . scared the old lady shitless." He stopped his annihilation of a head of iceberg and turned, knife pointed, to look her over. "I'm an ass man myself, know what I mean?" His leer bordered on the grotesque.

"Me, too," Bea said sweetly. "How long did you know Willie Shep?"

"A hijacker yet. Who the hell would believe it? I was jumping the old lady when the heat knocked. Christ, if I don't perform a couple of times a week she thinks I'm playing around. Course, she's right, I like a little variety. You ever fool around? About three months is all."

"You knew him three months?"

"Which is two months and five weeks too long. God, you shoulda' heard the scream Marilyn let out when he grabbed a handful."

"Willie made a pass at someone here?" Bea fought for coherence and wished for an interpreter. But then, who would interpret the interpreters?

"Pass, smash. Mar was back here on a break, and Willie walks up behind her, one hand gives a goose and the other grabs a knocker. Jesus, did she yell. Everyone in the store stopped and pissed."

"That's when they fired him?"

"Boss here don't give a fuck, you know. Hell, no union, and they can give you the finger anytime. Mar knocked him cold with a blue."

"A blue what?"

"A frozen bluefish. Thought she nearly killed the little bastard."

"Did you ever see him with any of his friends?"

"Dudes like Willie don't got no friends. They're professional enemies. I mean, you can't go to the local for a beer and a shot with Willie. He'd be hitting you up for five and you never could make out."

"You never saw him with anyone?"

"Blond bird came in a coupla times and they came back here and yelled at each other. Like she wanted him to lay a few on her, but he never had any money—always broke."

"Who was she?"

"A tough little bitch. I tried a play or two the first time she waltzed in, but she was the kind would want you to lay a C-note on her before she assumed the position."

"Did you ever see him read anything such as books or newspapers?"

"Little fink couldn't read the price list and get it right."

77

"Did he ever talk politics?"

Jimmy O'Halloran finished sprucing the last of the iceberg and carefully hung his rubber apron on a nail. He jockeyed the crate of produce onto a dolly, snaked a comb from his back pocket, and slicked his hair back. "Break time. How about you and I going back behind the avocados? We got a mattress back there for when Mar's in the mood."

"How about me telling your old lady?"

He blanched. "You wouldn't do that?"

"Then you wouldn't have to perform for maybe six months or a year."

"You wouldn't do that?"

"Don't tempt me, Jimmy. Really, don't tempt me."

Bea found a symmetry to Willie Shep's career. She backtracked his job history and found that before the three months at the supermarket there were three months at the taxi company (fired after a minor accident when it was found he'd been drinking on the job). Then there was the loading dock at the wire mold factory until terminated for excessive absenteeism. In none of her interviews had she discovered any political awareness on the part of Willie, any evidence of radical literature he might have read, or radical friends he might have had. At least not as far as his jobs were concerned. She knew from the police dossier that he'd spent a year in the Marines before being given a general discharge, which she knew was a euphemism for a goof-off the service wanted to dump.

The sign that read ROOMS stuck in the parlor floor window of the brownstone on East Tenth Street was flyspecked. Bea climbed the steps slowly. Her feet, even with the comfortable shoes she'd worn for walking, were beginning to have that dull numbness that pressages a full ache. With a sigh, she reached for the heavy knocker and let it fall three times in rapid succession. The dull thud echoed through the interior of the house.

A high voice penetrated the door. "All right, all right, keep your pants on."

The woman who finally opened the door was of indeterminate age and very round. By some strange quirk of obesity, her stomach had moved outward and upward to meet the pendulous sag of her breasts.

78

This provided a surface that made any evidence of a waistline indiscernible. She looked at Bea with small eyes embedded deep in a round face.

"Your sign says rooms available."

The chain clattered off its hook as the woman leaned out the door to peer sideways at the sign in the window, as if viewing it for the first time. When she glanced back at Bea her eyes moved down the pantsuit.

"You want further uptown."

Bea began to feel that she should pay more attention to her dress. An early morning pass by a produce clerk had now been followed by her identification as a prostitute. "I'm interested in a room on the second floor rear."

"Don't allow no men unless he's your steady."

"I doubt I'll have visitors."

"Why that room?"

"I heard about it."

"You don't look like a cop."

"I want to see Willie Shep's room."

"Cops already cleaned it out. I ain't running no tour guide service."

"I'll pay a week in advance."

"It ain't cleaned up."

"I want it the way it is. I'll pay two weeks in advance."

"Forty bucks."

Bea slipped two twenties from her wallet and winced. How many times had she criticized Lyon for spending money this way? "Can I have a receipt?" A round eyebrow was raised on a round face. "I guess it's not important." She followed the landlady inside. The house smelled. Its inhabitants undoubtedly used hot plates, and a strange mixture of past cooking odors permeated the dimly lit hall. The landlady stopped at a rear door on the second floor and pushed it open.

"Like I said, it ain't been cleaned up or nothing. But you don't care about that, do you, honey?"

"Not really."

"I heard of your kind. Get your kicks this way, don't you? Comin' in a dead man's room and thinking about him getting his head blown off. You're really into that, aren't you?"

Bea cocked her head and smiled. "You ought to try it sometime."

"Weirdo. The city's full of them." The round woman turned away in disgust and painfully made her way down the stairs.

Bea stepped into the small room and shut the door behind her. She estimated the room to be approximately fifteen feet square with a high ceiling. It had undoubtedly been divided off from a larger room when the brownstone was converted to a rooming house. Its one dirty window overlooked a refuse-filled small yard in the rear, and beyond that a slat fence separated it from a furniture warehouse. Only a small bit of sun would ever peek through the upper portion of the window. A frayed white curtain hung on each side of the window, the lower part of which was frayed, as if some prior occupant kept a cat.

The furnishings were equal to the room: an iron bedstead of ancient vintage with lumpy bedding, a bureau, and a worn overstuffed chair. She examined the top of the bureau where the contents of the drawers had been dumped. She gingerly went through the items: a few pairs of socks, handkerchiefs, a wallet-sized photograph of a two-year-old boy, and little else. She turned and began to examine minutely the remainder of the room.

In twenty minutes Bea was back downstairs knocking on the door of the parlor front apartment. "Go away. I'm watching my soaps." She knocked again. Louder.

The door snapped open as the round woman glared at her. "Will you go back upstairs and do your kinky bit and leave me alone?"

"I want to see his other things."

"What other things?" The round woman's eyes narrowed to tiny apertures.

"The things you took from the room."

"I didn't take nothing. Anything's missing, the cops got it."

"I know what the police have, and there are other belongings of Willie Shep's around here somewhere."

"Get outa' here!" She attempted to slam the door, but Bea stuck her foot inside and winced as it caught her instep.

"I can get the police."

"He owed me back rent."

"I just want to look."

"No cops?"

"No cops."

Bea followed her into a small bedroom. With a grunt, the landlady bent and pulled a cardboard carton from under the bed. "He owed me. I ought to get something."

Bea stooped and began to go through the box: a small portable television, cuff links, a sport jacket.

"There was a pawn ticket in there for a watch, but I sold it."

"Why didn't you pawn the TV?"

"Don't work so good. It keeps rolling."

Bea nodded as she opened a small metal box. Inside were several papers, the documentation of a short life: his general discharge from the Marines, unemployment compensation forms, a court service for child support. She read that one carefully. Willie Shep was charged by one Loyce Bolton Shep for back child support for one minor child in the amount of $710. Odd, the police report didn't mention a wife. She closed the box thoughtfully. "Did he ever have visitors?"

"Never. Except once a dirty blond girl came. They had an argument and were yelling so bad I had to go up there and ask her to leave."

Bea picked up more photographs of the little boy and one of a girl with long hair. "Ever see him read anything?"

"Never. You can have the box and everything in it for twenty."

"Thank you," Bea said as she stood. "I'm quite finished."

The address on the court document in Willie Shep's belongings took Bea to the West Side of Manhattan. The cab left her at the corner of Seventy-fourth and Amsterdam, and she walked a half block down Seventy-fourth. She recognized the architecture of the dwelling as Stanford White, built over eighty years ago. Its career had followed the course of the city as the neighborhood's complexion had changed.

She passed through a marble portico and rang the bell over a smudged card that read LOYCE BOLTON. The door immediately buzzed open and she stepped into an ornate hallway with a graceful staircase that wound toward the next floor.

A woman's voice yelled down from the top of the house. "Up here on the third floor. Leave them by the door."

"I'm not the grocery boy."

"Who is it?"

Bea continued plodding up the marble staircase without answering.

At the second floor she glanced up to see a woman peering over the railing above. Long blond hair hung over the side of a pinched face with a pouty mouth.

"I don't know you."

"I'd like to talk to you for a few minutes, Loyce Shep."

"Why?"

"About your husband."

"Oh, shit!" The face disappeared from the railing, and as Bea reached the third floor a door down the hall slammed. She knocked without answer, but continued knocking until a muffled voice called out, "We're separated. Go away!"

"You know what happened to him?"

"Go away!"

"Do you want me to announce it to the whole building?"

The door opened and slammed against the wall as a hand reached toward Bea and pulled her into the apartment. "Come on, lady. Nobody around here connects me with that guy." The door was closed and double latched. "How'd you find me anyway?"

"The court papers."

Loyce slapped her forehead. "I knew it. I knew it. I shouldn't have taken him to court. Fat lot of good it did me anyway."

A single naked light bulb burned dimly in a kitchen area to the right of the doorway, and Bea had to squint in order to make out the features of Loyce Shep. She was perhaps twenty-two, although the mold of her face was already beginning to harden. The deepening crow's-feet around the corners of her eyes were nearing a permanence that in a few years would give her a perpetually petulant look. The figure was thin to the point of gauntness, with small pointy breasts poking at the T-shirt she wore tucked into spattered jeans.

Loyce pushed a strand of hair away from her eyes and shook her head. "So, what do you want?"

"To talk about your husband."

"He's not my husband anymore. We hadn't lived together for two years, and the only reason I didn't get divorced is that I didn't have the bread."

"There's no need now, is there?"

"It was the best news I had all week. Grab a chair or, should I say, pillow and I'll get some coffee."

Bea stepped into the still darker living room and halted in the doorway. The walls of the room were painted black, the window was draped, and the furniture consisted of pillow groupings around a low coffee table where a candle in a red globe flickered. "It's interesting decor," she finally said.

"It's wild when you're turned on. Hey, you want a joint?"

"Not just now, thank you."

They sat on pillows around the coffee table as Loyce served coffee in cracked cups. A heavy scent of incense filled the room.

"I know he's dead and all that—but this widow bit is something new for me. There ought to be something in it for me somewhere."

"Sell your story."

Loyce leaned toward Bea over the flickering candle. "That's you, huh? You dug it up about Willie and me, and you want the inside story of how it was."

"Yes, I want information." There was a whimpering sound in the far corner. Bea's eyes had adjusted to the dark room, and she could now make out a playpen shoved up against the wall. A white face peered over the top bar as small fingers clenched the pen railing. "Your baby's awake."

"The kid's always awake."

"How long did you live with Willie Shep?"

"Two rotten years. He gave me a story, you know. When we met, he told me what a big deal he was. I was a kid and didn't know any better. We met in this disco place over in Yorkville, and he told me he was a Wall Street broker. And, the sap I am, I believed him. You know what he really did? Can you imagine? He was a runner. You know, one of those guys that go all over town carrying stock certificates in little bags. Minimum wage he was getting, and even that didn't last long until he was canned."

"Why did he get fired?"

Loyce shrugged. "Who knows? Why did he ever get fired?"

The baby began to whimper, while Loyce looked annoyed.

"What sort of people were his friends?"

"Ha! What friends? We never had no one over except a few of my old girl friends, and later even they stopped coming."

"Did he read anything?"

"Sure. Lots."

Bea leaned forward. "What?"

"Comic books. Bugs Bunny, Superman, stuff like that." The baby's whimpering became louder until Loyce got to her feet and went to the kitchen. She returned with a piece of white bread that she flipped into the playpen. "So, what else? You want to know about our sex?"

"Do his parents live in the city?"

"Both dead. He was half raised in foster homes. That's another thing. I could tell you the lies he told me about his old man that would make you bust a gut."

Bea Wentworth did not want to know any more about the short unhappy life of Willie Shep. The day's interviews had been sufficient, and she felt this avenue of investigation was now closed. Willie, by any report she had come across, did not read radical literature, did not indulge in long talks with fellow terrorists, had few if any friends, and had lived a life of utter failure.

Bea got to her feet and automatically held out her hand. "Thank you very much for your information."

"Hey, what about paying me for my story?" The baby began a more incessant cry.

"Is your baby a boy?"

"The kid? A boy. Looks like his father," she said impatiently.

Bea went to the playpen and reached forward with both arms. Round eyes stared up at her from an immobile face. She reached under the armpits of the child and lifted the surprisingly light weight to her chest. She made low cooing sounds as the baby's arm wound around her neck and a wet face sniffled against her breast.

She had held her own child like this years ago, and the memories of the tiny child's arms around her neck were—and then a bicycle and a car—and she and Lyon had never returned to the house on the Green again.

"Perhaps he needs a bottle," Bea said as she stepped around the corner of the arch into the kitchen area.

The swaying naked light bulb hanging from the ceiling hovered over the child and he blinked as Bea looked at the thin body. "Oh, my God!" The damp diaper was the only clothing over the rail-thin body. Burns dappled the skin around the upper arms and down across the stomach of the child. A misshapen arm groped for Bea.

"Gimme' the kid!" Loyce snatched the child and returned him to the playpen.

"Those are burns."

"When he cries it annoys my boyfriend."

"His arm . . .?"

"Kids fall. What's it to you?" the blond said defensively.

"Have you seen a doctor?"

"The kid's all right."

Bea fumbled with the door latch and let herself out into the hallway as quickly as possible. She clattered down the marble steps with eyes brimmed with tears.

A shrill voice called after her. "What about my story money?"

The desk sergeant looked at her without expression.

"I said a case of child abuse."

"Try the hot line."

"How do I do that?"

He wrote a number on a small pad and handed it to her. "There's a pay phone down the hall."

The voice who answered the emergency number at the Child Abuse Center was a replica of the sergeant's. Bea succinctly recounted the facts concerning the Shep child followed by the address and apartment number. "Will you get someone over there within the hour?"

"Lady, I'll be lucky to get someone out there within the month."

"The baby's in danger."

"Try the local precinct."

"That's where I am now."

"I'll put an urgent on it, but we've got budget problems, you know."

"I know," Bea said with resignation. "Do the best you can. Someone should get over there tonight."

"Lady, that would take a personal order from the mayor."

Bea hung up and leaned against the wall. The day's activities rushed over her in a wave of fatigue. She left the police station and gave her waiting cab the address of the Algonquin Hotel.

Within twenty minutes she had checked into the hotel and fallen across the bed. She thought she'd sleep for an hour or two, then order a sandwich from room service and place a call to Lyon. She closed her eyes.

The look on the child grasping her neck stood before her in a clarity more sharp than the light in the black apartment. She sat up and reached for the phone, dialed the long-distance line, and then a Connecticut exchange.

The voice that answered was slightly irritable, which seemed typical of the day. "Henry, this is Bea Wentworth. Let me speak to the governor."

An extension was picked up almost immediately. "Beatrice! How are you, hon? I was thinking about you this afternoon during a conversation with Glasgow."

"Governor, do you know the mayor of New York City?"

"Beatrice, no politician knows the mayor of New York if she can avoid it."

"The governor?"

"We meet in conferences from time to time. He's okay."

"I want you to do something for me, Ruth. Tonight, please. A real personal favor."

"Anything for you, Bea. Well, almost anything."

Bea quickly recounted the story of the Shep child. When she had finished there was a pause on the other end of the line. "Let me understand this," the governor said. "You want me to call the governor of New York who is to call the mayor of the city who is to call the commissioner to send a social worker ..."

"Within the hour."

"To some address on West Seventy-fourth Street."

"Yes, Ruth. That's what I want."

"It's very important to you?"

"Very."

"If this weren't an election year ..."

"You'll do it?"

"I'll do it," the governor said. "But, please, not too many of these."

For the hundredth time Willie Shep moved down the bus. Lyon gripped the gun in a sweaty palm. The face on the approaching hijacker seemed made of sand as the features flowed across a bare skull, changing in ever continuous patterns until merging into a malevolent grin as he stopped by the seat in front of Lyon and aimed. Lyon fired through the newspaper and watched again as the skull flew apart.

He awoke with a start. His neck was cricked from the uncomfortable position on the easy chair in the Herbert living room. The half-finished coffee on the floor beside him was cold and blotched. As he pushed himself erect, the myriad aches from the balloon accident telegraphed their presence in short shooting pains. He felt two hundred years old.

It was the phone that had awakened him, and he lurched down the hallway toward the telephone table.

The house was quiet. The small sounds that signal occupancy were missing. He was alone except for the Murphysville police cruiser stationed in the driveway with the young patrolman and his shotgun. It had been a fitful day peopled with nightmares that marred spasmodic sleep.

Bea's note, pinned to clean clothes piled neatly by the sofa bed, had disturbed him.

> Lyon—here are clean things. Stay in bed as long as you can. Do not leave the house. Repeat. Do not pass go. The watchbird is watching you. I have gone to New York for some shopping. Love, B.

It seemed an odd time for her to purchase a new winter wardrobe.

He picked up the phone and felt a twinge in his elbow that had escaped earlier notice. "Yes."

"For the man who's supposed to be the best, you're sure screwing things up, Wentworth."

"Who is this?"

"Cut the coy bit. My friends in the Big Apple tell me you missed Nick."

"Nick who?" It was unmistakably the same voice as the other call.

"What I don't understand is, why didn't you take him out when you blew away the punk?"

"How come you're so sure I'm your man?"

"I appreciate your cover, but it's been blown. You've been doing jobs for us for ten years now, and you're the only one we work with that uses a forty-four Magnum."

"I think we ought to meet."

"That's a switch. It must mean you have the merchandise. The old man says that every day with the stuff loose is dangerous. He's authorized me to pay you a bonus when Nick is out of the way and you deliver the merchandise. He's worried, and I don't like him worrying. You have a week, Wentworth. A week to take care of things, or somebody you don't know comes looking for you."

The phone went dead in Lyon's hand and he slowly hung up. He had thought the first call was possibly a crank, but now with the second, it all began to make a little sense.

# 9

"... A week to take care of things, or somebody you don't know comes looking for you."

They sat quietly for a moment in Rocco's office after the recording of the phone call ended. Rocco's feet thumped to the floor as he pushed off his swivel chair and began to pace in front of Lyon, Raven, and Sean Hilly. His arms made short chopping motions. "Who the hell is that joker?"

"Seems to me that the somebody he is going to send after Lyon has already arrived," Raven said.

"How's that?" Hilly asked from his deep slouch in a side chair.

"I'm thinking about the rigged balloon accident."

"I'm not altogether sure I like my phone calls bugged, Rocco."

"It was my own phone."

"Then how did he know I was there?"

"I wanted to cover all the angles. After the first call we put an intercept out at your place. When he called Nutmeg Hill the second time I had the policewoman on duty answer and give him my number."

"Could you trace the call?"

"Not nearly enough time."

"Right after my unknown friend called, Bea telephoned from New York. She's checked into the hijacker's background and is convinced that he didn't have any political motivations."

"We have that recorded, too."

Lyon frowned. "Pardon me, I'd momentarily forgotten I was being monitored."

Hilly changed the angle of his slouch. "It's the usual bit, then. All the hijacker was after was the money. Out-and-out greed."

"And some skewered notion about what life owed him. Bea's assessment is good enough for me." Lyon began to pace as Rocco slumped back in his chair. "We know more than we did."

"How's that?"

"We thought the first phone call might have been a crank, the second proves it wasn't. The caller is convinced that we have a connection."

Raven looked at his notes for a moment and then stuck his pen behind his ear. "I have always thought I was as imaginative as the next man, but this is confusing. The caller thinks you're working for him, and if you don't get Nick in a week he'll send somebody after you. But somebody has already tried to kill you in the balloon. It's upside down."

Lyon stopped by the window and looked out over the tree-shaded street leading toward the green. "If we make a basic assumption or two, it all begins to make sense. Let's assume that the phone caller hired a gunman."

"Gunman?" Hilly snorted. "You don't hear that word on the street anymore. Say somebody put out a contract."

"A contract on the man called Nick."

"In that case, the hit man is the one who gave you the gun."

Raven sighed and put away his notes. "What about the mysterious Major Collins?"

"Seems to me that the bus is getting awfully crowded," Hilly said. "A hijacker who kills people, a hit man, and a target."

"The hijacking was a coincidental event that acted as a catalyst. I lean to the theory that the man who gave me the gun is the hit man and Collins is the target. I was given the gun so the killer wouldn't have to expose himself."

Rocco drummed his fingers on the edge of the desk. "I don't know. That could be it, but it's hard to believe that he'd blow up a bus to kill all the witnesses and also try and take you out on the off chance you might recognize him."

"It fits if the killer thought the target was on the bus that morning. The death of the others was unimportant to him. He wanted to get one specific person."

"That brings it back to you."

"No, not yet. He was trying to kill Collins, but Collins left the hotel early that morning. A fact that was unknown to everyone except the two New York detectives on duty at the hotel."

Rocco looked thoughtful. "And you roomed with Collins that last night."

"There's no secret about that. Now, at that point the killer assumes that Collins told me something, perhaps it concerned what the caller refers to as the merchandise."

"Which is what?"

"If we knew that, we'd know the answer to almost everything."

"So he tried to eliminate you on the chance that you know something. That Collins told you something that night. Which is what?"

"Damned if I know. He's certainly sure by this time that I can't identify him."

"You said that Collins knew who you were."

"Yes, he had bought one of my books for his grandson."

"What about your other interests?"

"I mentioned hot air ballooning to him."

"No, I mean your past involvement in certain investigations."

"He mentioned it briefly, almost offhandedly."

"Did he give you any sort of message?"

"If he did, it wasn't anything recognizable."

"Is it possible?"

Lyon reviewed the short conversation that had lasted only a few minutes in the hotel room. "He admitted that he was not an army officer, and then went on to say he was involved in a war of another sort." Again, he went over in detail the conversation and the signing of the book. The inscription before his ... "There was something written in the book, something about the secret of the karst followed by a little drawing."

91

"What in hell does that mean?"

"What about the drawing?" Hilly injected.

"It seemed a private thing, so of course I didn't ask."

"Do you remember it?"

"Vaguely. It resembled a microscope drawing of a blood vessel, but not like any I've ever seen. And yet, it did look like something I'd seen before, but it eludes me for the moment."

"And you think everything ties into those two phone calls?" Hilly asked.

"Yes, and they make a good deal of sense in a certain context. Let's say the caller hired a hit man but doesn't know his identity. He sees newsreel footage of the bus at the aftermath of the hijacking, he can identify the target, and knows that a forty-four Magnum is always used. Then my name appears as the one who shot the hijacker with a forty-four."

"Which makes him positive that you're the one with the contract."

"And now there's a bonus for returning what he calls the merchandise."

"Okay, the caller is convinced Lyon is the hit man, while on the other hand the real killer thinks he got Collins on the bus and now wants to eliminate Lyon on the chance that Collins told him something that night in the hotel room."

"It puts me in the middle," Lyon said.

"I would say so."

"I don't like Bea alone in the city under these circumstances." Lyon started for the door. "I'm going after her."

"Not without backup you aren't."

"I'll go with him," Hilly said. "When we get to the city I can get him all the protection he needs."

"You got a piece?"

Hilly flipped open his jacket to reveal a holstered service revolver. "Ready for bear."

"Raven?"

"I don't ordinarily carry a weapon. I did hoist an M-16 on a couple of trips in Africa when we were in dangerous country, however . . ."

Rocco shook his head. "Are you going with them?"

"Oh, no. I thought I'd check in with Kim and get some more background. I'll leave the other stuff to the professionals."

"Fine." As Lyon and Hilly left, Rocco picked up the phone. "Get me Captain Nesbitt in New York," he told the switchboard. While waiting for his connection, he impatiently drummed his fingers on the desk. "One hell of a liaison man you are," he said half aloud. He looked pensive, and when the phone rang he snatched it up. "Nesbitt? Rocco Herbert here . . . the chief in Murphysville . . . right . . . I have some news for you on the bus case, but first, about your liaison man up here . . . Hilly. Sergeant Sean Hilly who you sent up here to sit on my shoulder . . . Hilly, damn it! . . . What do you mean you didn't send any liaison man?"

"We could have gone by the motel and picked up my vehicle, Mr. Wentworth." Hilly turned the pickup onto the Connecticut Turnpike access ramp.

"Lyon, please, Sergeant."

"Right. Call me Sean." He accelerated the truck to sixty and frowned as the frame vibrated until he reduced the speed to a more moderate fifty.

"Probably should replace this thing, but we use it mostly as a balloon chase car, which explains the radio and four-wheel drive."

"The doorman at your wife's hotel will flip when we pull up." He thought of the long bramble scratches along the body of the truck. A moving cloud path released rain in windblown sheets that speckled the front window. Hilly fumbled for the wiper control and flipped them on.

The dashboard lights cast a glow around Hilly's chin and covered the lower part of his face in a dim light. The upper part of his face was in shadows, which gave him a slightly ominous look. Lyon studied the New York sergeant. There was something familiar about him . . . the man with the gold badge. . . . No, it couldn't be. He was getting paranoid to the point where he had begun to suspect the most unlikely individuals. But still . . .

"You live on the Island, Sean?"

"Yep."

"You said you have a split-level. I would suppose a wife and children go along with that?"

"Boy and girl, ten and fourteen. Even have some of your books in the house. One of them about queer-looking animals."

93

"The Wobblies."

"Yeah, I guess that's them." He lapsed into silence.

"Have you worked with Nesbitt long?"

"Nesbitt? I'm new on the task force and don't know many of the guys." He glanced over at Lyon. "If I didn't know better, I'd think you were questioning me."

"Didn't mean it to sound that way," Lyon said, which wasn't actually the case. The truck's forward momentum was cut drastically as it pulled into the right-hand emergency lane. "Something the matter?"

"That tollbooth ahead," Hilly leaned forward and brushed the misted windshield with his sleeve. "Bunch of cops are stopped—like they're forming a roadblock."

"Oh?" Lyon rolled down the side window and stuck his head out. The rain had begun to slacken, and a mile ahead he could see the toll station with a line of cruisers parked in front of several booths, forcing traffic to funnel through two toll stations where troopers peered into each car. The pickup slowed to a stop. "What's the matter?"

"You said this hulk had a radio." The voice was cold.

"Under the dash. We use it for communication with the balloon."

"I don't give a damn what you use it for." He fumbled with the CB set. "Does it get police calls?"

"Yes." Lyon's hand inched toward the door handle as Hilly located the police band and tuned it in. "I want to get to the city."

Hilly didn't answer, but kept one hand on the radio while the other flipped open a button of his jacket.

"Car Nineteen. I have subject vehicle on the south lane near the Murphysville toll station."

The pickup jerked ahead as Hilly threw it in gear. Lyon pushed down the door handle and levered his body across the seat. "Stay put! Close the door." Hilly had drawn his revolver from the clip holster at his belt and had it pressed against Lyon's side. He swung the truck in an arc across three lanes. The pickup left the highway and careened down a grassy slope of the divider. As the truck reached the culvert at the bottom, he slammed it into four-wheel drive and drove up the other side into the northbound lanes.

Troopers ran for their cars.

"Goddamn heap!" Hilly snarled. "Why don't you have a decent set of wheels?"

"It's been adequate."

"Aw, shut up!" The truck vibrated as it approached seventy, and at seventy-five Lyon thought it would literally fly apart. There were now three cars behind them with sirens and flashing dome lights. They were gaining rapidly.

With an abrupt movement of the wheel, Hilly turned the truck toward the road edge, battered through a wire guard rail, and began to push up a brushy slope. In tanklike fashion, it plunged through small brush and knocked down saplings.

As their forward momentum carried them through a heavy mass of foliage, a large tree loomed ahead, only a few feet from the nose of the truck. Lyon braced his legs and threw his hands before his face as they struck the tree. The impact threw them both forward against the dash and windshield.

Dazed, Lyon fumbled for the gun and received an elbow in the midsection.

Hilly lunged from the car and then turned to level the muzzle of the pistol at Lyon's forehead. Several state troopers left their cars at the bottom of the hill and ran toward them with drawn guns.

The gun barrel touched Lyon's head. "You know, Wentworth, you really should get it."

At the bottom of the slope, Rocco Herbert pulled his car off the highway and wedged it between two state cars. He found Norbert standing in the headlight glare of one of the empty cars.

"What's up?"

"He has a gun and just ran into those trees. My men are after him."

"Lyon?"

"Still in the truck."

They began to trot up the hill toward the disabled truck. As they approached it, they saw Lyon slumped against the dashboard. Rocco tugged at the door, which the force of the collision had jammed shut. He cupped his hand against the window and looked toward the still form of his friend. He braced his feet, and grasped the handle with both hands and tugged. With a whine of screeching metal, the door opened and he reached for Lyon's shoulders.

Norbert's flashlight spilled across them as Rocco levered Lyon from the car. As he did, Lyon stood. "Are you all right?"

"He had the gun six inches from me . . . I thought he was going to shoot. He didn't, but why?"

"I don't know. I did find out that he's an imposter."

"That doesn't surprise me."

"We've got him, Captain!" Norbert turned his light toward the trees where two troopers, supporting a handcuffed Hilly between them, emerged from the brush.

"Is he clean?"

"Is now." The first trooper handed a revolver to Norbert.

The captain looked down at the gun and then at Hilly. "Let's see that ID you're so proud of."

"In my back pocket."

The second trooper took the wallet from the prisoner's pocket and handed it to Rocco. Rocco glanced at it a moment. "This is what he showed me in my office the day he arrived."

"All right, Hilly, or whatever your name is. You going to make it easy on yourself, or do you want it the hard way?"

Lyon stood before the one-way glass and looked into the interrogation room at the state police barracks. Flanked by Rocco and Norbert, Hilly sat at a table nervously sucking on a cigarette. The reels of a recording machine turned slowly.

Norbert cleared his throat. "This is Captain Henry Norbert. Also present are Chief Rocco Herbert of the Murphysville force and a man representing himself as Sean Hilly of Long Beach, Long Island."

"I don't represent anything. That's my name."

"You have been read your rights. Would you like me to repeat them?"

"I know my Miranda."

"The police identification you carry and showed to Chief Herbert is a forgery."

"No, it's real."

"There's no Sergeant Sean Hilly listed with NYPD."

"I was on the force until two years ago."

"You resigned?"

There was a long pause as Hilly stubbed out his half-smoked cigarette. "I was kicked off for being on the pad."

"They bring charges?"

"They let me resign. Otherwise I couldn't get my investigator's license—which I got, along with a permit for the gun."

"You still misrepresented yourself to Herbert."

Hilly shrugged. "My client said that would be the best way to get in tight. Who the hell figured some boonie cop would check with New York?"

"What client?"

"Privileged information."

"Are you dumb or just stupid? We're talking more than a dozen counts of murder one here."

"Murder? You got to be crazy."

"A busload of people."

Hilly shot to his feet. "Like hell! You got me on impersonation, some traffic counts, maybe a little assault on Wentworth; what's this with murder?"

"Someone blew up that bus and now we know who."

"Bullshit! You're looking for a fall guy, and it's not going to be me."

"Who's your client?"

Hilly looked blank and then sank back in the chair. "I don't know. I honest to God don't know."

"That's a dumber answer than before."

"I got a phone call. The guy said he thought Wentworth was holding some valuable merchandise of his, or else knew where it was. He said that's why Wentworth was carrying a piece on the bus that day. He wanted me to get in tight, stay close to him, and report back."

"And on the basis of a phone call like that, you agreed? Come on."

"He followed it up with a typed letter and two thou in cash. Hell, I needed the money. The fuckers are foreclosing on my house."

"How do you report to this mystical person?"

"I write to him at a box in Tarrytown, New York."

"What box number?"

"Seven-two-four."

Norbert made a note on a legal pad. "We're going to check that out."

97

"Go ahead. I wrote one yesterday that should get there tomorrow morning."

"What's this merchandise you're looking for?"

"I don't know. I was just to report everything I saw concerning that jerk Wentworth."

"You expect us to believe that you accepted money from an unknown client for an unknown job when multiple murder was involved?"

"There wasn't any murder when I took the money. That bus thing happened when I was on my way from New York. Then it was too late. I'd already spent most of the money."

"Come on, Hilly. You expect me to believe that?"

Rocco left the interrogation room and joined Lyon behind the one-way glass. "Well, what do you think? Is he the guy who gave you the gun?"

"I don't know, but I would be curious to know if he ever wore a beard."

"I'll ask him when I go back in. You know, Lyon, it all fits with this fink. Suppose he's telling half the truth, and was hired by some unknown client . . . hired to hit someone. He admits he was on his way to Connecticut when the bus blew up. His story stinks, but it fits."

"The man who telephones me by name, he would have to be Hilly's client."

"Right."

"Find out about the beard, Rocco."

The large chief nodded and returned to the interrogation room. "You ever wear a beard, Hilly?"

"You're not going to screw me with that bit."

"We can find out, you know."

"So, what if I did. I was working narcotics when I was on the force. It made good cover."

"When did you shave it off?"

"I don't know. A couple of months ago."

A trooper corporal entered the room and handed Norbert a note. The captain left the room, leaving Rocco to continue the questioning. In a few minutes, Norbert entered the room where Lyon stood. With him were the two highway service station attendants Lyon had talked to the day the bus burned.

"You see that guy in there?" Norbert waved toward where Rocco bent menacingly over Hilly. "You recognize him?"

"That big guy?"

"No. The other one. Could he be the man you saw at the station talking to the tanker driver?"

"I don't know. It was like the other side of the apron. I only glanced at him."

"Take another look. Did you see him at the service station that day?"

Both men looked through the glass and then simultaneously shook their heads. "Not him," the first one said.

"Could be this guy," the second said as he pointed at Lyon. "He was there. I distinctly remember seeing him."

"Me too," the second agreed.

Captain Norbert turned red as he faced Lyon. "Wentworth, get out of here! Just get out of here!"

Rocco and Lyon sat at Sarge's place. The booths had been restored and the aura returned to its comfortable seedy ambience. Lyon drank his second sherry gratefully.

Rocco threw down a neat vodka and signaled to Sarge for another. "Norbie's never going to break that guy down. We're going to be stuck with that mysterious client bit until hell freezes over."

"Hilly fits the mold almost too easily."

"And that bothers you? Like he was set up?"

"In a way, but perhaps I'm being too suspicious. I have a feeling that the man we're looking for is careful, always careful. He's a devious man who has used disguises before. Also, what is the merchandise they're looking for? Why was a contract put out on the missing man?"

"Maybe Norbie has the answers."

"What answers? All I have is questions." Captain Norbert stood scowling by their table. "Can't you pick a better place for a conference than this dive?" He plunked into a chair facing the bar. "I thought the town went for a bundle on the new headquarters, Roc. Which, as I recall, includes a conference room."

"I don't like the color scheme, we don't serve booze at headquarters, and don't call me Roc."

99

Norbert sat rigidly in his chair. "What's the sign outside? Says topless." He peered toward the bar. "When they come on?"

"A little later," Rocco said and kicked Lyon under the table. "What's with the prisoner?"

"Initial check with New York says he's what he claims. Ex-cop, licensed private investigator, gun permit in order, bad credit rating, and a wife and two kids on the Island. We've booked him on half a dozen charges. Your wife's on the way home, Wentworth. New York will escort her to the Connecticut line and my men will pick her up from there."

"Thank you. What about the post box in Tarrytown?"

"Like Hilly says. He's mailed four letters and there are four letters there. We have it staked out, but I'm not hopeful. It's going to be a long case. We have to place him near the bus. It'll take time, but we'll nail him."

"Motive?"

"He was paid. He admits that."

"By who?"

"We'll get that information too—eventually."

"Give me a lift home, Rocco. I want to be there when Bea arrives." As they walked to the car, Lyon gave a last look over his shoulder. Captain Norbert still sat rigidly at the table—waiting. "How long before Sarge tells him that the dancing girls have been canceled?"

"A long time," Rocco replied. "A long time."

# 10

Lyon Wentworth made drinks badly, but worse, he kept forgetting the orders.

"A pink lady, martini, two stingers, and a scotch and water with twist," a voice called to the kitchen.

He looked at the array of bottles spread across the kitchen table with their accompanying trays of lemon twists, olives, and maraschino cherries that he had laboriously laid out before the cocktail party started. He reached at the scotch, hesitated, and tried to remember the sequence of the order shouted through the kitchen door. What in hell was in a pink lady? He began to search for his bartenders' guide.

Nutmeg Hill had been transformed. Cars lined the lawn and crowded the drive as a hundred people spilled through the house and out onto the patio where a professional waiter and bartender worked a portable bar. Lyon glanced through the window at the bartender on the patio. He was immaculate in white jacket and tie and held a cocktail shaker over his head which he shook with zest. They should have hired two bartenders.

Through the kitchen door he could see Bea in the living room, moving from one group to another with her head thrown back in laughter. One hand held an untouched glass of ginger ale, while the other was perpetually extended in greeting. A banner stretched across the room printed in wavering block letters that read OVER THE TOP WITH BEA. It was the last fund raiser of the campaign, and carefully planned with the utmost cynicism—pour on the drinks before the impassioned appeal for money to finance the final radio and television spots. It was hoped that, as in the past, checkbooks would be produced and checks written. For the unprepared, a supply of blank checks and BEA WENTWORTH FOR CONGRESS pens were available.

Lyon watched Bea in a corner talking with Maximus Popov and the blond girl he lived with. It was a seemingly benign scene, which made him wonder why he worried. Hilly was under arrest charged with the crimes of impersonation and assault. The combined forces of Connecticut and the city of New York were working to create the case necessary to charge him with the murders. It would be time-consumming and difficult, but they would probably succeed. So why was he worried about one of his wife's supporters who coincidentally happened to be present at the balloon accident? Why did he still doubt Hilly's guilt?

He dialed Rocco on the kitchen phone.

"Sounds like you've got a bash going on there."

"Should have come."

"On my salary I couldn't contribute a quarter to Bea's campaign, but tell her luck. And besides, you don't know the work involved in applying for all these grants. Papers up the kazoo."

"I appreciate your difficulties in obtaining your helicopter, but could you check something for me?"

"From past experience, that means you probably want to send me on a jaunt to Alaska."

"Not this time. After the bus caught fire, the state police must have taken the names of all witnesses. All those from nearby cars, the service station, and the restaurant."

"Sure. I have a list here that Norbie sent over."

"Anyone we know on it?"

"Let me dig it out."

Lyon glanced back into the living room while he waited. Bea had moved from Popov and his girl friend, and the bearded balloonist looked his way and waved a hand in greeting.

"I've got it," Rocco said. "We know a lot of them, mostly rest area employees who live in Murphysville. A good many of the others are out-of-state people."

"Anyone else?"

"Let me look. You know, Lyon, if Hilly were there, he probably used a false name. Any killer would."

"Not if he were from this area and might be recognized."

"Your buddy Max Popov is on the list."

"He is?"

"Hell, so are sixty other people. Does it mean anything?"

"I don't know. Thanks, Rocco." He slowly hung up and walked back to his bar mixings, trying to remember the drink requests he'd been working on before the call.

"I once did a great piece for *Esquire* on the making of the true martini through the use of Zen." Raven leaned against the door holding his cocktail glass upside down.

"I assume that means I don't have the proper transcendental qualities to my barkeeping?"

The writer gave a sad shake of his head as he moved behind the bar and searched through the tray of martini olives. "First, one must find the proper olive. A fruit—or is it a vegetable—that holds the true essence of all olives." He selected a small one and held it up between thumb and finger. "You see before you an example of absolute perfection in olives." He plunked it into a glass and held the gin bottle high over the shaker and let a thin stream of the clear liquor pour into the cocktail pitcher. "Now, let the shadow of the vermouth fall across the shaker. Notice that the actual presence of the alien wine is not required, merely the essence of the vermouth."

"I think your Zen manual is trying to say that I make them too weak."

"Strength is not the requirement. Perfection is the goal."

"Should the essence of vermouth falling across the pitcher be chilled?"

"You mock me, sir." Raven tasted the newly mixed martini and sighed. "Now, there is perfection of nothing less than pure grandeur."

"Can you make a stinger?"

"But of course." He quickly began to mix the drinks. "Anything else?"

"Let's go for a pink lady and a scotch and water with twist. Don't know how you remember them all." Raven mixed the drinks efficiently.

"Well, as Chief Herbert would say, you've got the bad guy in the slammer, what's next?"

"You mean Hilly?"

"He always did look suspicious to me. Those little eyes sunk in a criminal face."

"They haven't formally charged him with murder, but that's the direction in which they're moving. Makes a rather neat ending to your article, doesn't it?"

"I couldn't ask for more. The Wentworths in their white hats triumph again. I must get some shots of you and Bea at home. Some casual but homey pics. You working on a book in the study, Bea in her garden, that sort of thing."

"Then you'll be returning to the city?"

"No, I thought I'd do the actual writing here in Murphysville. A sort of flavor-of-the-scene type of thing." He finished the round of drinks, drank his own, and made another.

"I've never sold anything except children's books. I suppose that with articles like you write, you only sell the North American serial rights?"

"I suppose." He busied himself with the bartending as Kim entered the kitchen and sampled Raven's martini.

She coughed. "Lord! A few of these and you'll be doing handstands on the widow's walk."

"He says they're Zen martinis."

"I'll bet. Back home we called that straight booze."

Raven took the glass back from Kim and tasted it with a slow smile. "It's a developed taste."

"How's it going out there?"

"One more round of drinks and we'll put the touch on them."

"By the way, Raven, where are you staying? The Dell Motel?"

"I moved from there. Now I'm just down the road a piece. What can I make you, hon?" he asked Kim.

"Down the road?" It was then that Lyon noticed that Kim's hand lying gently on Raven's with that casual touch of intimacy that men and women have only when they sleep together. "Oh."

"My place," Kim said and looked directly at Lyon as if to challenge him.

"Why not?" Lyon smiled at her. "Where's the sherry?"


Maximus Popov was at the far end of the patio near the parapet overlooking the river. He had a small entourage surrounding him as he pointed skyward and explained certain fine points of hot air ballooning. His blond girl friend stood to the side looking slightly bewildered. Lyon beckoned to Popov who immediately moved away from the group to join him. He grasped Lyon's hand.

"You're looking great. You've evidently pretty well recovered from the accident."

"Ribs are still taped, but otherwise I'm whole. Mind if I ask you something?"

"Go ahead, except that if it's about those leaking propane tanks, I still haven't been able to find out how it happened."

"About the bus ..."

"The one that burned and killed all those people. I was there, you know."

"In the service station or restaurant?"

"The men's room. Which tells you why I pulled in there in the first place. When the bus went, right after the explosion, we all ran outside, but it was obvious that we couldn't help anyone."

"You know, Max, whenever we're together we seem to only talk about ballooning. You teach economics, don't you?"

"Yes. I'm supposed to be some sort of expert on foreign exchange and arbitrage." He looked out at the setting sun casting sheets of red along the river. "I could make a hell of a lot more money in the city in private industry, but who wants to leave this?" He gestured expansively over the valley.

"Do you travel a lot?"

"I do a good deal of consulting work for large corporations with foreign interests." He turned away from the setting sun. "Are you interrogating me?"

Lyon laughed, but found that his voice lacked any ingenuous quality. "Come on, Max, you're a fellow aeronaut."

"Who was at the balloon meet when you almost died and who also

105

was at the scene of the bus fire. By God, Lyon! I think you're making me some sort of suspect."

"They have this man Hilly under arrest."

"But you think he didn't do it?"

"I didn't say that."

"You know, old man, it's not very good manners to invite a friend to a fund raiser for your wife and then accuse him of murder."

"I didn't accuse you of anything."

Popov turned and walked away. "You didn't have to."

Lyon walked through the devastation of the party's aftermath and shook his head. Nutmeg Hill was a shambles that now resembled a Barbary Coast bar after three whaling ships had disgorged their crews for their first leave in two years. He didn't recall any fistfights or dancing on tables, which might have explained overturned chairs, broken glass, and dozens of partly consumed drinks. He began to empty overflowing ashtrays into a lawn bag.

Raven Marsh was slumped over the kitchen table sound asleep, while Kim chortled happily in the study as she listed the night's receipts and totaled them on a pocket calculator. When he reached the patio with his bag, he found Bea at the parapet looking out over the night.

"Seemed pretty successful," he said as he emptied a particularly distasteful ash collection into his container.

"God, I hate asking for money."

"It's part of the system. Do you know any other way?"

"I haven't been able to come up with one yet. You know, Lyon, I fib a bit. They ask me my stand on a particular issue, and if I know their predilection is contrary to mine, I fudge a bit or become evasive. I don't out and out lie about how I feel, but I come damn close to it sometimes."

"You must be one of the few politicians who don't lie."

"I hedge."

"Do you know any other way?"

She turned with a tired smile. "I haven't come up with the answer to that one either. What did you say to Popov? He left rather abruptly in a huff."

"He seemed to resent my asking him about his coincidental appearance at the bus accident."

"Oh, Lyon, it's over! They have Hilly in jail. Do you have to insult our friends?"

"I didn't intend to be insulting. Did you know that Kim and Raven are having an affair?"

"Where have you been the past few days? It couldn't be more obvious."

"Has she talked to you about it?"

"No, and I haven't asked. It's too new. She's still unsure and uncertain over whether it's a transient thing or one more lasting."

"I wonder about him, too. That business about *Playboy* magazine . . ."

"Why don't you call Rocco and have him give Raven the hose treatment or whatever they use these days? Kim would love that. However, I'll save you a little time. There isn't any contract with *Playboy*. Kim passed that on to me. Raven concocted that in order to gain access and get our cooperation. He's evidently been having trouble with editors because of his drinking and has been blackballed from a few magazines. He thinks that selling the article about us will get him back in good standing."

Lyon looked through the kitchen window to where Raven was slumped over the table. "I don't see much movement toward reform."

"That's Kim's problem, not yours."

"You let him go!"

"Not me. The state police." Rocco Herbert picked up a file from his desk and admired a photograph. "You know, I think I'll get a duck."

"A what?"

"This kind of duck." He handed Lyon a photograph of an army amphibious craft. "Government's offering them cheap to law enforcement agencies. If I write my grant application properly, I might swing it."

"Spare me. Right now, I want to hear how Hilly got out."

"It's one of your liberal, bleeding heart, pinko deals called bail."

"How much and who paid it?"

"Ten thousand put up by a bail bondsman for the usual percentage."

"That seems lenient for all the charges against him."

"He was licensed to carry a gun, he didn't actually kidnap you, so what they had on him is still bailable."

"How about material witness?"

"He didn't witness anything that Norbie can prove."

"He's still involved in murder."

"You know that, I know that, the state prosecutor knows that, and Mr. Hilly knows it. But the guy still claims he was legitimately hired."

Lyon sat dejectedly. "Somehow it doesn't seem right."

"I can go down to Sarge's place and recruit a seedy lynch mob."

Lyon looked sharply at his friend. "Since when did you join the forces for constitutional rights? I seem to recall a few incidents when you really bent things."

"Call it facing the inevitable. All right, this one is a murder case, yesterday it was a bicycle. Not that I equate the two, but the problem is the same. Jamie Water's new ten speed was ripped off from in front of the Congregational Church. I found it stashed in Herbie Smith's mother's garage. Herbie claims he bought it from a guy for ten bucks. We all know Herbie stole it, but I can't get a warrant."

"Receiving stolen property."

"Sure, and I throw Herbie's seventy-year-old mother in the can." Rocco studied the architect's rendering of the new station that hung on the wall. "Through quirks in federal and state grants I've got enough equipment to fight a minor war, but there's something wrong and I don't know the answers."

"Okay, if we can't solve the problem of law and order in this country, I'd like to get on with finding two missing bus passengers. What's the latest?"

"Norbie's been in touch with New York. There's no trace at all of the man who gave you the gun. He's disappeared into the proverbial thin."

"What about the one who called himself Collins?"

"Last seen leaving the hotel that morning."

"He was coming to New England. I think that he'd continue, perhaps by another means of transportation."

"They covered the airlines, trains, and bus depots."

"Rental cars?"

"They're pros, Lyon. The news photo glossy has been shown to rental car people throughout the city. Hell, he could have hitchhiked, had a friend drive him, or for that matter, still be in the city."

"Then there are no leads at all?"

"They thought they had one, but it fizzled out. An airport limo driver thought he recognized the photograph."

"Did they follow up?"

"Of course they did."

Lyon stared at the ceiling. "If you get me the name of that limo driver, I'll start there."

"You'll start nowhere."

"What?"

"In the first place, what makes you think you can do something the combined forces of Connecticut and New York can't do?"

"Sometimes I have an intuitive sense about things."

"Like the time you were the only junior officer ever to argue with General MacArthur at a staff meeting."

"I was right, wasn't I? The Chinese did cross the Yalu."

"And you received the fastest discharge on record. And besides, I can't protect you if you leave Murphysville."

"That explains why you had Officer Martin wandering around the cocktail party last night with a flat beer in his hand."

"I'm shorthanded because of vacations. Play it cool and we'll turn up something."

"As long as we had Hilly there was a chance, but I'm not seeing any forward movement."

"It's not your problem."

"Yes, it is," Lyon said softly. They peopled his dreams and haunted his everyday thoughts, and always would until it was over and he had fulfilled his responsibility to them. "I'm going, with or without your cooperation."

Rocco looked at him steadily. "I was afraid you would. I'll get the name."

The homogeneity of the borough of Queens was a startling thing to Lyon. The streets of identical row houses, each with small front plots fenced by low chain link fences with three steps to the stoop, had an antiseptic quality that he felt sure must affect the dreams and aspirations of the occupants.

The cab stopped midway down a block. "Here you are, buddy."

He paid the driver and walked through the gate of number 3333, crossed the tiny yard, and climbed three steps to ring the bell. A vacuum cleaner ceased its whining hum as the door opened to the extent of the chain lock.

A gaunt, slightly jaundiced face of a woman of middle age peered through the opening. "Whatcha' want?"

"I'd like to see Mr. Coin. Billy Coin who works for Carter Limousine."

"He ain't here."

"They told me he was off today."

"Who you collecting for?"

"I'm only trying to locate Mr. Coin."

"He's at the neighborhood."

"Isn't this his home?"

"The neighborhood, the neighborhood. Don't you understan' English?" She brushed a wisp of hair from her forehead with a tired gesture.

Lyon turned from side to side to look down the rows of identical yards. "It seems to be a fine area."

"The bar. The local, you know? Henny's around the corner on the boulevard. Go in all the way to the back. You can't miss him, mister, you sure can't miss him."

The door was shut with a note of finality and Lyon retreated down the walk and turned toward the boulevard. His empathy for the woman behind the chain lock filled him with an ennui that he attempted to dissipate by striding quickly toward the main thoroughfare.

The opaque front window of the "local," or Henny's Bar and Grill, contained two beer signs, a sloppily printed ERIN GO BRAGH, and a large paper cutout of a green shamrock. Lyon entered and coughed at the overwhelming smell of stale beer.

A half dozen men and one lone woman sat at the bar with draft beers and an occasional shot before them. Half looked at a wall TV playing "The Price Is Right," while the other half looked across the bar at faraway places unseen by others.

Lyon ordered a sherry and asked for Billy Coin.

"In the back. You can't miss him."

A gargantuan laugh echoed from the rear of the premises and Lyon followed the sound. A pool table under a wide hanging lamp dominated the room. A fat man, the owner of the laugh, held a cue stick in triumph while his opponent, a smaller man in overalls, uttered low curses.

"D-fucking-vastation," the fat man bellowed. "You're dead, Charlie."

The thin man scratched his final shot and hung his cue in the rack with a disgusted snort and went to the bar. Billy Coin laughed again in short guttural snickers.

"Mr. Coin, may I speak to you a moment?"

"Play pool?"

"Only a little."

"Rotation. Dollar a ball."

"Mr. Coin, I really . . ."

"Listen, buster. This is my day off. This is my time away from the old lady. So I have a couple of pops and shoot some rotation, right?"

"I guess." Lyon took the first cue from the rack and chalked as Billy Coin racked the balls.

"Dollar a ball and I break."

"Please do." He watched the fat man remove the triangle and sight. "I wonder if you'd look at a picture I have, Mr. Coin?"

Lyon's remark coincided with the shot. The cue ball slithered to the side and hit limply to the right of the number one ball. Coin turned to him with a reddened face.

"D-fucking-pressing. Can't you keep quiet?"

"Of course." Lyon saw that he had a good shot at the first two balls if he banked properly with a little English. He handed the glossy print of Collins to Billy Coin and lined up his shot. "Have you seen this man?"

"Take your turn," the fat man said impatiently.

As best Lyon could remember, the last time he had shot pool was years ago in an officers' club in Seoul when the liquor ran out. He took the shot.

The cue ball slonked the two ball into the far right pocket, spun, and hit the one resolutely into a side pocket. He turned away from the table with satisfaction.

Coin's jaw dropped and his voice lowered four octaves. He lay the end of his pool cue along the top of Lyon's hand. "We don't like hustlers in Henny's, buddy. Last guy tried that got his fingers busted."

Lyon knew that his shot was one of astronomical luck, perhaps the first piece of true luck he'd had since the whole thing started. "Continue the game, Mr. Coin. A dollar a ball, or shall we double our bet? Or would you rather just talk to me a few minutes?"

The fat man wiped his forehead with a handkerchief and signaled for a drink.

"We'll call it a draw and talk."

They sat in a secluded booth where Coin looked at the photograph. "I already told the cops that maybe this was a guy I had on a trip. I couldn't be sure. You know how many trips I make a day to the airport and back? Plenty. Now, the airlines like us to watch out for the screw-fucking-balls in case they're possible hijackers."

"You work out of the East Side Terminal?"

"Make the run to Kennedy. Cops checked it out, what more can I tell you?"

"I understand they did a thorough job."

"You talk funny for a cop."

"I'm not." With dejection he realized that his slender lead had been well investigated. New York had probably mounted a thirty-man task force to check out rental agencies, airports, and bus terminals. And he had developed nothing further than they had. He had to do more. "Mr. Coin, the day you saw this man on your bus was twelve days ago. You were working the seven-to-three shift. He probably boarded the limousine in the morning. Would you tell me about that day? From the first thing you did when you got up that morning."

"Crazy. Why should I?"

"Or finish our game."

"Get me a drink and tell me what you want to know."

Lyon got the fat man two doubles and had him relax in the booth. Slowly, softly, he led him through the day: his awakening, dressing, what he had for breakfast, the drive to work. It was a stumbling, seesaw affair, and perspiration popped out across the man's forehead as he tried to recall the day and all its minor events.

112

". . . second trip of the day. Musta' been about ten in the morning. He was first on. Real nervous, ordinary-looking guy. Never would have noticed him if he weren't shaking so bad. Dropped his book, picked it up. Sat right behind me. I remember that because on the Pulaski Skyway he had a coughing fit and I wanted to throw the bastard through the window."

"What?"

The fat man opened his eyes. "I told you the whole bit. He got off. He left. O-fucking-kay?"

"Pulaski Skyway?"

"How else can you get to Newark?"

"You work out of the East Side Terminal."

"That day I filled in for a guy at the West Side and took runs to Newark all day. Cross the fucking meadows and back again."

"Jersey," Lyon said. "Did the police know that?"

"Nobody ever askt."

The molded plastic contour seat was not made for comfortable slouching. Lyon stretched his legs forward, oblivious to the airport bustle surrounding him. There were three car rental agencies in the terminal, he had spoken to each, shown the photograph, and received a negative response from every clerk.

It had been presumptuous of him to think that in one day he could possibly achieve a lead that had eluded the police task force assigned to the case. He glanced up and looked toward one of the rental car booths. A large flight had arrived, and a cluster of businessmen with attaché cases hovered around the counter. No wonder the clerks could not recall one inconspicuous man over a week ago. And even that assumed he had rented a car. Perhaps he had flown out, met someone, never arrived here in the first place. Placing any credence in Billy Coin's hazy recollection was probably a mistake.

But that was all he had. Lyon closed his eyes and pictured the hotel the day of the hijacking. After dinner Collins had come to his room, they had a drink together and a conversation that lasted five minutes. As he again reviewed the short dialogue, he knew that there were more things he didn't know about Collins than he did know. His name wasn't Collins, he was not an army officer, he did not live where his ID said he did. What did he know about the man? Someone was trying

113

to kill him and since he traveled under an assumed name, he must know this. He had also bought a children's book to give to his grandson, and that grandson was the object of his trip to New England. Yes. Collins had continued on, but how?

The dead ones were part of the milling crowd. Lyon did not believe in vengeance as such, but there had to be a balancing of the scales.

If he could assume that Collins came to Newark Airport to rent a car, he would undoubtedly want to cover himself as much as possible, but would have had to use a credit card. The airports would obviously be covered by the man's pursuers. What would Lyon do in that case?

He'd leave Billy Coin's bus outside the terminal and take public transportation to the nearby city of Newark. Another obstacle thrown in the path of anyone following.

Lyon left the waiting room and hurried toward the parking lot.

He waited until the customer at the rental agency booth in the lobby of the Newark hotel was taken care of before he approached the clerk. Her name tag said to call her Debbie, but she seemed a little too old and tired to be a Debbie. She gave him a slight grimace which he returned with a smile as he handed her a copy of Collins's picture.

"It would be a great help if you could tell me if you remember renting a car to this man."

"I'm sorry, sir. I really can't help you. I don't remember."

"When you rent a car, if it's not to be returned here, is there a notation on the form where it will be returned?"

"We have to know when and where our cars will come back."

"Could you look up for me, the day of the sixth, what cars you had signed out for Springfield?"

"Aw, come on, mister. I'm tired. My feet hurt, and my break comes up in five minutes."

He opened his wallet and slid a fifty-dollar bill across the counter. Bea would kill him. "I'd be most appreciative."

Her hostess smile returned. "I'm not that tired." She stooped to rummage through a file cabinet beneath the counter and pulled out a stack of forms that she placed on the counter. Sorting through them quickly, she pulled one from the center of the pack and put it aside. "None to Springfield that day."

"Are you sure?"

"I'll look again." She flipped through the day's slips and then shook her head.

"I'm sorry. The only sign-out that day to anywhere in New England was one to Hartford, Connecticut."

"None to Springfield . . ." Then he wondered about a man who lied about his name: would he tell his real destination? He was going somewhere in New England, somewhere where the bus stopped. "May I look at the Hartford one?" She turned the form so that it faced him. He scanned the details and saw that a Floyd Collins had checked out a red Plymouth Volare, marker number New Jersey S34543, for Hartford and used an American Express Card to cover the rental. "Can you tell me if this car has been returned yet?"

"In a sec." She punched some numbers into a small computer terminal. "No, it's still out. Due back the day after tomorrow."

"Thank you."

The man at the far end of the hotel lobby, with the newspaper in front of his face, lowered the paper. He waited until Lyon left before carefully folding the paper and walking toward the rental car desk.

# 11

"THIS IS AN EXERCISE IN FUTILITY."

Lyon spread the city of Hartford street map across the card table in his study and used a straightedge to mark it off into squares. "It's the only futility we have left."

Bea took the Magic Marker from his hand and made a rapid calculation. "If I take the population of the city and divide it by one car for every four people, that means there are forty thousand cars in Hartford. And that doesn't even consider the possibility that it could be parked in some garage."

"Garages are usually filled with people's own cars. Visitors park in the drive or street."

"It's such a slim lead. We could spend a week looking for a car that we're not even sure belongs to the right man."

"He took back the marker and continued dividing squares on the map. "It's the only thing I know of to do."

"If I told you I was driving to Hartford, I could also mean one of the dozen suburban towns around it. Are we to check them out too?"

"If we have to."

"When do we start?"

"Right now."

She sighed. "Okay, only keep my area away from the state capitol. I am supposed to be working today."

The city of Hartford has a population of slightly less than 150,000, but with its surrounding suburban environs, there is a statistical area of close to 800,000. Lyon knew this, and although he had tried to sound positive with Bea, if they were not able to find the Plymouth Volare in the city itself, they would be facing a nearly impossible task in the remaining time they had left. He could only hope that the car was still within the city limits and parked somewhere visible.

They divided the city in half. Lyon took the northern sections, Bea the southern.

That night Rocco Herbert shook his head as the dejected pair recounted their lack of success. "Were you able to cover most of the city?" They nodded. "Did it ever occur to you that he might have taken the car out to go somewhere?" Again the affirmative nod. "Why didn't you come to me in the first place?"

"I hate to bother you, Rocco."

"Amateurs," Rocco said as he reached for the phone. He talked in a low voice for a moment and then dialed another number. "Rose? How are you? Rocco Herbert. Is Pat around?"

Lyon smiled. Sergeant Pat Pasquale of the Hartford Police was an old friend of Rocco's, and had helped them before on several occasions.

"What are you doing home, you guinea bastard? Stuffing your face with pasta? . . . If Rose hears you using that language she'll . . . Need a favor, Pat . . . Yeah, I'll give your kids a ride in the helicopter. . . . A red Plymouth Volare with Jersey plates, marker number S34543. . . . No, I'm not calling you at home about a hot car. I only want to know where it's parked. We'll take it from there. Urgent, Pat. I'll give your kids a ride on the duck. . . . No, duck . . . with a *D*." He hung up and turned to them. "Pat'll call the watch commander and have the word put out on this shift and also on the twelve to eight. If it's there, they'll find it."

Lyon answered the phone so quickly before the completion of the first ring that Bea only made a low sound and turned over in bed. Pat

117

works fast, he thought as he pulled the receiver to his ear.

"Wentworth?" It was the voice from the other calls, but its quality had changed so that the intonation of his name implied a latent menace.

"Yes?"

"I got your letter. I told you we'd pay a bonus for the reels, but this is extortion. But the old man is willing to go along and pay the hundred thousand on delivery. Do you have them yet?"

"No."

"I don't like delays. Time is running out and the old man is sick. Foul up and we get you. Remember, I know who you are."

The line went dead. Lyon hung up and lay back on the pillow. Sleep disappeared as he looked into the darkness deep in thought.

Pasquale called Rocco at seven the next morning. Rocco immediately called Lyon and gave him the address. At eight the Wentworths were on their way to Hartford.

"I passed this house yesterday," Bea said. "I'm sure the car wasn't there then."

Lyon glanced at the red Volare in the driveway of the three-family house and checked the license number against his notes. "He must have been out with it. Well, let's go." He left the car and started up the walk toward the front door.

"WENTWORTH, COME BACK HERE."

"Huh?"

"This is a three-family house and we don't even know the real name of the man we're looking for. Or are you going to pretend you're a census taker and . . ."

"He's got a grandson between six and ten."

"How do you know?"

"That's the age group for the Wobbly books." He walked briskly up the street to where two little girls were playing hopscotch on the walk. He talked to them a few moments and returned to lean in the car window. "There's a seven-year-old boy who lives in the ground floor apartment and whose grandfather from Florida drives the red car."

"Do your informants know the name of the granddaddy?"

"Grandpops, but I don't think that's much help."

The curtains had been removed from the window on the front door and they could see into the apartment. Cardboard cartons were strewn across the living room and some were filled or partially filled with the knickknacks of everyday living.

"Looks like someone is moving in or out," Bea said as Lyon knocked.

A woman in her late twenties wearing a man's large white shirt with the tail tied at her midriff and paint-spattered dungarees moved into the living room and waved at them. "Open Sesame. Come in. It's not locked." As they stepped into the cluttered apartment she moved around them with dancelike steps and pointed to various cartons. "There's this stuff in here, and there's more stuff in the other rooms. Don't know where it all comes from. All the furniture goes except the stove, thank God. We'll have a built-in stove at the new place. What do you think?" She turned toward them expectantly with arms akimbo and a fey smile below wide, ingenuous eyes.

"I'm afraid we're not the moving company."

"I thought you were the estimators. Uh oh, I know you two."

"You do?"

"Listen, guys. I bought two copies of the *Watchtower* last week. Which is really two more copies than I really need. I'm really sort of busy, okay?" She smiled again and Lyon liked her.

Bea stuck out her hand and the woman automatically grasped it. "I'm Bea Wentworth and this is my husband Lyon."

"Wentworth? Sounds sorta' familiar."

"I met your father during his trip north. He made me promise to stop in if I got to Hartford."

"Pop isn't here right now. He took Mark for a walk. They ought to be back soon. Can I get you some coffee or something? If I can find a pot."

The apartment was designed in semirailroad fashion. A tiny vestibule into the living room, behind which was a dining room, a short hall with two bedroom doors, and then the kitchen to the rear.

"You're obviously moving," Bea said.

119

"Yep. Tomorrow the moving van comes for us, and Pop flies to the old country. Did he tell you what he did for us?"

"I think he meant for it to be a surprise," Lyon said, still wondering if they were in the right house.

"He bought us a wonderful condominium out in the country. It has everything: swimming pools, tennis courts, woods. No more worry about that old dinosaur who lives upstairs yelling at Mark or traffic in the street."

"That's just wonderful," Bea gushed in her best political manner.

"The old country. That's Yugoslavia, as I recall?"

"Don't let Pop hear you say that. It will always be Serbia to him."

The relief was so powerful that Lyon sank on the couch and almost crushed a model airplane. "Your father bought one of my books for Mark and had me autograph it. I hope your boy liked it."

"Hey, that's where I know your name! Wentworth. Sure. You write those Wobbly books. Pop said he met the guy who wrote them." She turned to Bea with the same exuberance. "You're Beatrice Wentworth. You're running for the Senate or something."

"Congress."

She vigorously grabbed a startled Bea's hand. "I'm going to vote for you, Mrs. Wentworth."

Bea laughed. "I appreciate support wherever I can find it, but I'm afraid my district stops at Murphysville."

"Hey, coffee, you guys? I think I have some leftover Twinkies."

"Coffee would be fine," Bea said. "Without any Twinkies, thank you."

"Sure. One java and hold the Twink." She laughed and turned to Lyon. "You, Mr. Wentworth?"

"Coffee would be great."

"Back in a flash." She disappeared into the kitchen as Lyon shook his head affirmatively. He liked the young woman whose apartment they were in and the freshness of her exuberance. He only hoped that whatever came of this caused her no harm.

A partially packed carton of books on the living room floor before the couch was still unsealed, and resting on top was a copy of *The Wobblies' Revenge*. He took it from the carton, turned to the inscription, and read it again:

To my beloved grandson Mark. May he one day understand the secret of the karst and why it was necessary. Your loving grandpops.

It was written with the small handwriting of an accountant using a fine-point pen. Below the signature were the small rows of strange symbols:

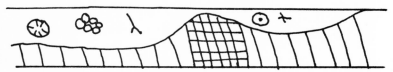

He closed the book thoughtfully and replaced it in the carton.

"Here it is." She returned to the living room with three mugs of coffee. A small edge of Twinkie protruded from the corner of her mouth, while a dab of cream filling stuck to the tip of her nose.

"I hate to say this. I remember Mark's name, but not yours."

"Hey, my fault. I'm Darlene. Darlene Whipple." She stuck out her hand again. "I'm twenty-eight, have one child, and am divorced. My husband—my ex, that is—said it was like trying to live with a box of Wheaties." She laughed. "I never did figure that one out."

A series of sharp knocks on the lower part of the front door made a quick passing frown flick across Darlene's face. "That must be Mark." She opened the door and knelt to hug and pat a sniffling seven-year-old. "Hey, little guy. It's all right. Where's Pops?"

"He left me and I was lost. I didn't know how to get home until I saw the school." He wrapped his arms around his mother until the tears quickly dried and he looked over her shoulder with wide eyes at Bea and Lyon.

"Lyon," Bea said.

"I know." He crossed quickly toward Darlene and the small boy and stooped next to them. "Mark, tell me what happened to your grandad. It's very important."

Darlene looked puzzled.

"We were walking along and a man came in a car and got out. My grandpop told me to run home and he got in the car and left."

"You had better call Pat and Rocco."

"Where's the phone?" Bea asked Darlene.

"In the kitchen. Hey, what's going on, guys?"

Bea was halfway through the dining room when she stopped. "I don't know his name."

"What's your father's name?"

Darlene stood and held her son protectively. "Hey. I thought you were his friends. What's going on here? If this is some sort of flimflam . . . I don't have much flim to be flammed out of. Huh? Okay?"

"I think you had better tell us his name and find me a photograph of him very quickly," Lyon said softly.

Kim stood by the fireplace and dominated the living room. She held papers in one hand, while the other pulled her reading glasses to the tip of her nose so that she could glance from her notes toward Bea and Lyon on the couch. "Recently," she read, "Secretary Wentworth stated that she is some sort of modified socialist." She took off her glasses and shook her head. "My God, Bea. Why didn't you just come right out and endorse Karl Marx?"

"That's not what that means, and you know it."

"I do, but your opponent has seen fit to capitalize on it, if you'll pardon the pun. May I proceed?"

"I'm sure you will anyway."

Kim read further excerpts from her notes. "We need a state income tax in order to increase social services."

"I'm running for Congress, not state office. My views on state taxes are not a question here."

"But they are, hon, they are."

"A shambles, huh?"

"If we'd found Nikola Pasic today it would be over and Bea could give proper attention to the campaign," Lyon said.

Kim looked puzzled. "You've lost me there. I thought we were talking about Bea's campaign. Who is Nikola Pasic?"

"AKA Floyd Collins."

Kim put her sheaf of papers on the fireplace mantle in resignation. "So much for politics. Next question. How do you know Nikola wasn't picked up by a friend? Maybe they wanted to go to a bar or a dirty movie. Who knows? Just that they couldn't take the boy along."

"From the little I know of the man, I'm positive he wouldn't leave his grandson alone on a strange street. Unless he had to."

"Then he was kidnapped."

"He's been gone for fourteen hours so far."

"Does his disappearance make any more sense than the rest of it? What do you know about him?"

"Pat's checking with Florida," Bea said.

"What do we know?" Lyon mused. "A man who traveled from Florida in a roundabout route under an alias. He was born in the city of Nis in the Serbian province of Yugoslavia, became a naturalized citizen in the forties, and worked for twenty years as a bookkeeper for a Florida company. His wife died of cancer last year, and he has one daughter whom we saw today in Hartford. He seems to have a good deal of money, but that could be from a life insurance policy on his wife. He planned to return to Serbia for an early retirement. As innocuous a life as anyone on that bus."

"With the exception of one passenger."

The phone rang and Kim left to answer it in the kitchen. They could hear her voice, which was obviously raised for their benefit. "Wentworth campaign headquarters, where the elite meet defeat . . . uh huh." She reappeared in the living room. "Super pig would like to talk to Sherlock Holmes."

Lyon picked up the phone with dread. "Yes, Rocco . . . I was afraid of that. . . . Can't the daughter do it? . . . Of course, I know where it is."

His face was ashen when he returned to the living room. "They found Pasic's body. For reasons best known to the medical examiner's office, they don't want the daughter to make the identification."

The Chief Medical Examiner's Office for the state of Connecticut is in the University of Connecticut Medical Center in Farmington, a town a few miles west of Hartford. It took Lyon forty minutes to make the trip. When he arrived he found Rocco and Pat in the parking lot waiting for him. They didn't speak as they entered the building containing the morgue. Pat nodded to the attendant, and they were led to the body storage area.

Lyon had never been in a morgue before, and expected that in this modern, new building, and with modern antiseptic techniques, that there would be no smell. He was wrong. The cloying smell of chemicals and death assaulted him. They were taken to a white tiled room with a stainless steel refrigerated chamber pocked with numbered drawers. The assistant medical examiner pulled open number 10.

Rocco and Pat stood aside as Lyon approached the corpse.

It was the man he had met in the New York hotel room, the man he now knew was Nikola Pasic.

He stepped back in revulsion. "My God! What happened to him?"

"Is it him?"

"Yes, but the condition of . . ."

"Multiple burns over the thorax and groin surfaces of the body," the ME intoned. "Probably used a cigarette lighter. Death by strangulation."

"The wire was still around his neck when we found him," Pat said.

"He's been tortured."

"Yes," the M.E. said as he slid the body back into the refrigerator chamber. "The wire went back from his neck and was looped around his feet. It took him several hours to die."

The lights in Darlene Whipple's apartment were out as Rocco and Lyon parked in front of the three-story house. As Lyon walked reluctantly toward the front door, Rocco called after him.

"I'll wait for you, and we can go down to Pat's office and make our statement together."

Lyon nodded and continued up the steps to knock on the door. He waited and knocked again. The uneven shadows in the dark living room set off a subliminal alarm and he cupped his hands around the edge of his eyes and pressed against the glass.

Street light fell through the room and spilled across overturned packing cases that were now strewn haphazardly around the room. The faint light illuminated the edge of the couch he had sat on earlier in the day. It had been ripped with a knife and stuffing pulled from the cushions in large handfuls.

He elbowed glass from a lower pane and reached inside to unlatch the door. "Darlene!" He stumbled over the mess in the living room and fumbled along the edge of the dining room wall until his hand stuck a switch that lit an overhead light. He called again and ran for the bedroom hallway.

124

She was naked. Her frightened, hurt eyes stared up at him as he picked up a still lit overturned lamp. Her arms and legs were tied to the bedposts and a broad expanse of tape covered her lower face and mouth. Burns crisscrossed her body in streaks of red welts.

Rocco shouldered past him and slashed his pocket knife at the bindings. Lyon tore the bandage from her mouth and pulled her gently against him. Her breath came in short gasps and then she began to cry.

"In . . . in closet . . . Mark, . . ." she gasped.

Rocco found the little boy tied and gagged in the closet, released him, and handed her a terry cloth robe that hung there.

She folded the small boy in her arms as they sat on the edge of the bed swaying and gasping. She looked up at Lyon. "A man, at the door. I thought it was Pops until I saw the stocking over his head. He tied us up. Searched the house."

Lyon looked around the room and found that it had been thoroughly ransacked, drawers spilled on the floor, the mattress slashed, holes were even punched in the plaster wall. "I see."

"The spools. He kept asking where the spools were. Then he tied me to the bed. . . ." Her voice trailed off as she looked up at Lyon with wide eyes. "My father . . ."

Lyon sat next to her and the small boy and held them both in his arms.

He closed the door and stood for a moment with his back against it. The IV stand cast a crooked shadow toward his feet. She lay stiff and rigid in the hospital bed with her arms by her side and a blanket pulled deep under her chin. She seemed smaller than he remembered, as if the events of the past hours had wilted her, not only her natural exuberance, but also her stature.

"Darlene," he called softly.

Her eyes opened. Facial lines he'd not noticed before cut tracks of fright. "Who is it?"

"Lyon Wentworth. May I talk to you?"

"I don't want to talk." Her voice was flat.

He pulled a side chair toward the bed and sat in it silently. She continued looking at him without movement until her eyes blinked open, glazed from the effects of sedation. She fought to keep them open, as if afraid that the horrors would return if sleep overcame her. He reached out to hold her hand.

"It's going to be all right."

"Where's my baby?"

"Sergeant Pasquale took him home with him."

She sat up and he pushed her back. "The police . . .?"

"If I know the Pasquales, your only problem is that Mark will come back to you plump as a partridge."

A wan smile flickered briefly across her face. "What happened to my father?"

"He was murdered."

"Oh." Her eyes widened as if she were assimilating the fact and considering how much she might trust Lyon. "I suppose it was because he had a great deal of cash on him. I know he had several hundred dollars."

"No, I don't think it was that. They found his wallet. Someone was looking for something more important than a few hundred dollars."

"Which is why he locked Mark up and tied me to the bed."

"Do you have any idea what he was looking for?"

"He just kept asking for the spools . . . the spools, and when I'd shake my head no he'd bring the . . ." She turned away.

"I know how difficult it is, Darlene, but I want you to tell me about your father, particularly the last few years. We might come across something that will help us catch the man who did this to you and to your father."

With her head still turned she began to talk. At first in a hesitating, stumbling manner, and finally the words formed their own images and the dead man began to take on a distinctive shape.

Nikola (Nick) Pasic, as a very young man during World War II, had been deported by the Germans to work in one of their factories. Released at the end of the war, he had joined the masses of displaced persons roaming Europe. Finally obtaining passage to this country, he had landed in the United States in 1946. He had worked as a dishwasher and finally a waiter in Florida hotels while taking night courses at the University of Miami until he received his degree in accounting.

In 1950 he married Mary Lungsden, and shortly afterward Darlene was born. Her childhood, and seemingly the Pasic life, had been an average and uneventful one. They had always lived modestly, although Darlene knew that promotions he received while working for for the Hungerford Corporation could have enabled them to move into a more luxurious home. Her father had always been kind to her, although constantly fearful of losing his job and once again becoming a displaced person.

Darlene had married a serviceman and moved to Connecticut on his discharge. Last year her mother had died, painfully, of cancer, and this year her father had retired early with intentions of returning to Europe.

"He seemed to change after my mother died."

"In what way?"

"The desire to return to Yugoslavia, for one thing. He'd never mentioned that before. And he didn't want Mark and me to come to Florida and liv with him after my divorce. He got quite upset when I suggested it, even though he had the room with mother gone. I know he loved us, but it seemed as if he were afraid for us to be down there. He sent us money, and I told you about the condominium he bought for us. I didn't understand it."

"When he arrived in Hartford did he have any luggage?"

"No. He said he'd rented a car in New Jersey, and there'd been a mix-up on his luggage in New York. He was in the process of buying new things."

"Can you think of anything he said that was odd or out of character?"

She thought for a moment. "He was mostly concerned that I had enough money and that Mark and I would be all right. He said he would write us, but not to expect a letter until he got settled, which would be a year or so. Funny . . . he did say he was going to write one letter right away . . . to some important people here. I didn't know what he meant. When I asked about it, he wouldn't say anything. I'm not much help, am I?"

"You may have been. Why don't you go to sleep now?"

"I think I will."

Lyon kissed her on the forehead. Her wide eyes looked up at him and then closed.

127

He left the Murphysville police station and walked toward Main Street and the Green. There was nothing he could do for the time being, and he'd left word at the desk where Rocco could find him.

They were all busy. Rocco on the phone to the state police concerning Nick Pasic's luggage, and Pat Pasquale on the phone with the Dade County, Florida, sheriff's office. The youngest officer on the force, Jamie Martin, was sitting in front of the communications console at the front desk looking perplexed.

The Green was deserted. The white gazebo sitting in its center loomed before him as he walked across the grass and sat on its steps. He looked overhead to see an occasional star as clouds blew past in the path of a strong northerly wind.

In the ambulance on the way to the hospital, Darlene had told Pat that the stocking man had used her curling iron to burn her.

A curling iron? A small boy terrified in a closet. The dead in the flaming bus—what was worth such horror?

He looked over the quiet streets surrounding the Green. The historical commission required that the building facades remain unchanged, and the surroundings were as they had been a hundred years ago. It took little imagination to implant gas lanterns along the edge of the Green and see into the past. Men also killed in those simpler times. They killed, as they always had, for lust, gain, or ideology. Knowledge of which of these motivated the murderer was the primary step in locating Pasic's killer, and would be the mechanism through which they'd find him.

The police car jumped the curb and ran across the grass to swivel to a stop directly over a bed of tulips. Rocco and Pat slammed from the cruiser and trooped toward the gazebo steps where Lyon sat.

"Negative on the luggage," Rocco said. "The lab was able to identify Pasic's things from the bus and reconstruct the contents. There wasn't anything but the usual clothing and toilet articles."

"Whatever he was carrying could have been burned," Pat said.

"I don't think so," Lyon replied. "When Pasic talked to his daughter after he arrived in Hartford, he spoke of sending a letter to someone important. I think he intended to write to the FBI or the governor of Florida once he reached Yugoslavia. He was going to tell where the spools were hidden. He'd put them someplace safe."

"Florida has some interesting information," Pat said.

Lyon leaned back against the gazebo post. "The company Pasic worked for is connected to the Organization."

"How the hell did you know?"

"The man who's been calling me is willing to pay one hundred thousand for what Pasic had. Who else would pay that kind of money?"

"Right. Anyway, Nick Pasic, as he's known, worked for an outfit called the Hungerford Corporation. The Anti-Organized Crime Force in Florida has felt for a number of years that Hungerford is a primary outlet for laundering Mafia money by buying into legitimate business. It was a small local mortgage company until twenty years ago when it was purchased by some fronts. Then it began to grow by large infusions of mysterious capital. Today it's a major financial institution, loaning money and buying equity interests all over the country."

"Who's behind it?"

"They can't prove it, but they suspect Sergei Norkov."

"Who's that?" Rocco asked.

"The sick old man," Lyon said. "The financial mastermind behind all the families. Evidently he hasn't had any formal training, but for a man who picked up his knowledge of high finance on the street, he's a genuis. The Las Vegas skim was one of his minor innovations."

"And Nick Pasic was chief accountant for Hungerford."

"Any record on him?"

"None. He seemingly lived normally with a modest life-style. They did mention one thing."

"What's that?"

"When they checked Pasic's house, they found his cars still there and most of his personal belongings, but the house had been ransacked like someone was looking for something important."

Lyon stretched. "It all fits."

"How about letting us in on it before I book you for loitering in the park?"

"For whatever reason, Nick Pasic took off from Hungerford with the spools. They obviously contain information that is worth a good deal of money to someone, either recovered or destroyed. They hired a hit man to kill Pasic and destroy the spools."

"The killer picked up Pasic in New York and followed him to the boarding gate for the New England Express. He got on and sat directly behind you."

"The hijacking was a coincidence that fouled up his schedule. He probably intended just to follow Pasic and pick him up when he left the bus."

"When the hijacking occurred he passed the gun to you to stay out of the limelight."

"Yes. As I reconstruct it, Pasic left work, taking the spools. The word was put out and he was spotted in New York. Remember, probably every Mafia family in the country was after him. The killer was hired and trailed him to the bus line at Gate Twenty-nine."

"And he's cool enough to leave him in line and go have a drink?"

"The line at the gate was too short. He's obviously a man who feels that complete secrecy is important. He was willing to take the gamble that Pasic would board that bus."

"The next day he destroys the bus and all the passengers, thinking that he's getting Pasic and the spools."

"Except they weren't on the bus."

"Which he found out later."

"But why try and kill you? He knows you can't identify him."

"His initial assignment was to get Pasic and destroy the spools. He knew that I spent the night with Pasic and had become involved in the case. I had to be destroyed in order to preserve the secret of the spools. Later, when the bonus was offered for their return, he kept me alive to help him get to Pasic."

"Pasic was tortured before he died. He may have revealed their location."

"I don't think so. Pasic knew he was a dead man whether he talked or not. I think he held out, and that's why the killer went to Darlene's apartment after killing her father. He certainly wouldn't have done that if he had them."

"Then they still exist—somewhere?"

"And they're our answer. Not only important for what they might contain, but also because when we find them he won't be far behind."

"Hilly fits this situation completely."

"He might," Lyon said, and also thought about the bearded balloonist and economist, Popov.

# 12

"YOU'RE MAKING ME UPTIGHT, WENT-WORTH."

"I thought you'd rather talk."

"I'VE GOT TO HELP THEM FLY THIS THING. LET ME CONCENTRATE." Bea griped the armrests, braced her feet on the flooring, and pushed back against the cushion. The 727 shivered and then streaked down the runway.

He reached toward her right ear and adjusted the hearing aid. "Statistics indicate that flying is safer than driving on a highway."

"Statistics also say that flying to the moon is safer yet, but that doesn't mean I'm applying for astronaut training."

They were airborne. Lyon looked out the window at the retreating ground and tent-covered tobacco fields surrounding the Hartford Airport, Bradley Field. The plane banked toward the south and Bea gasped. She gasped louder as the retracting wheels thumped into their wells. "What was that?"

"The wheels."

"Do you know that ninety percent of all air accidents occur within two minutes of the airport?"

The loudspeaker crackled to life with a deep reassuring voice. "This is Captain Nelson. Welcome to Delta Flight seven-six-seven to Miami, Florida. Our flight time will be five hours and eight minutes. The temperature in Miami is eighty-four degrees."

The jet reached its assigned altitude and leveled off. The ground had disappeared in a fluff of white clouds. Lyon reclined his seat and leaned back to order priorities. His exact plans on arriving in Miami were still vague, although he did have letters of introduction from Rocco and Pat Pasquale. Also, explicit instructions from Rocco not to make any overt move without help and lots of it.

"There's a guy with the Florida Task Force named MacKenzie," the chief had said. "Gather all the info you want, but no moves without him—agreed?"

"Agreed."

There'd been a call early that morning from Pat. In an attempt to locate the spools, whatever they were, his men had searched Darlene's apartment, the new condominium, and any known place that Nick Pasic had been since his arrival in Hartford. Nothing had been discovered.

Rocco was to contact the American Express Company and get a list of all the recent credit slips submitted under the name of F. Collins. From them they might be able to track Pasic's route from Miami to New York.

Kim and Raven were driving to Florida, and along the way would check with the two major bus companies to see if Pasic's trip north had been by that means of transportation. They would also check with terminal managers in an attempt to see if Pasic had utilized lockers as a hiding place for the elusive spools.

Bea plucked at his sleeve, and he turned to see her deeply frightened face. "Croatian terrorists," she managed to mumble through stiff lips. "A couple of years ago they hijacked an airliner."

Lyon thought about that a moment. "No, I don't think so."

"YOU DON'T THINK SO! Here we're going to be blown to bits any moment, and you don't think so. Why don't they have parachutes on these things?"

"Really, Bea."

"Pasic was from Yugoslavia, right?"

"Yes, but ..."

"Those Croatians are fighting for independence and Croatia is part of Yugoslavia?"

"Yes . . ."

"And you're in deep."

"Bea, stop it. Pasic was from Serbia. Serbia is not part of Croatia. Prior to World War I, the Balkan countries including Serbia, Bosnia, and . . ."

Her hand went over his. "No, Lyon. No history lectures. I'll take your word for it, but now I have to concentrate on keeping the engines running." She clenched the armrests and closed her eyes.

The spools could be hidden anywhere. Perhaps they were miniaturized recording spools from a tape recorder. He had seen some that were hardly an inch in diameter. They could be buried, mailed, stuck in some niche. It seemed a nearly impossible task, but they had to be found for they held the answer to all that had happened.

Bea's eyes flicked open as the stewardess pushed the bar cart by their seat and leaned toward them. "I'll take a triple."

"I'm sorry, Miss, but regu . . ." The stewardess looked at Bea's pale face and silently arranged the drop table and gave her two ice-filled cups and four small martini bottles. Bea drank the first two quickly, relaxed a bit, and sipped at the second double.

"That doesn't look like a Zen martini."

"At this point in flight I'd drink vanilla extract if that's all they had. Speaking of Zen, things are getting heavy between Raven and Kim. Do you think they'll ever reach Florida?"

"They're only stopping at the major terminals: Washington, Richmond, Raleigh, and a few others. They ought to make it in three days. What do you think will happen between them?"

"I don't know. I worry about it."

"Mixed marriages are more acceptable these days."

"Not that. Marriage is still difficult under those circumstances, but Kim is tough enough to make it. I really can't put my finger on it, ᜍonly that I somehow feel he's conned her."

"He seems to be a nice enough person, although there is a touch of the con in him."

"I don't want to see her hurt."

"Kim is pessimistic about the campaign. How do you feel?"

Her eyes widened as she pursed her lips. "Campaign? What campaign? Am I running for something?"

"Last I heard, it was the United States House of Representatives."

"Oh, that campaign. The one where ten days before the primary my campaign manager is taking a slow motor trip to Florida with her boyfriend while the candidate flies to Miami with her husband to bask in the sun. Why am I here, Wentworth? Tell me that."

"I can't tell you how sorry I am about the time we're taking, but I have a strong feeling that before this is over I am going to need your help."

"Doing what?"

"Locating the spools."

"With the killer right behind us?"

"Probably."

"Which is why he's stopped trying to kill you. So you can lead him to the spools."

"As long as he doesn't have them, we're safe."

"If he's found them, he'll want you dead."

"Maybe."

"In which case, blowing up an airplane in flight would be an excellent method."

"It probably would," he replied offhandedly and immediately realized he'd said the wrong thing.

"Oh, my God!" Bea blanched and fumbled in the rack for the small paper bag.

The Hungerford Corporation was in a modernistic building located in downtown Miami. A gleaming white structure, with windows glazed as protection from the sun, it reeked of plasticity.

The young woman behind the reception desk seemed carved from the same material as the building's edifice. She smiled without feeling, looked coy without animation, and reminded Lyon of dancers he'd sometimes observed at the end of their routine when sheer will retained their smiles.

"Mr. Sergei Norkov, please."

She looked puzzled and then flipped through a wheel index. "Is he a new employee?"

"No, I would think he's been here for quite some time."

"Mortgages, leasing, or equity financing?"

"Perhaps all three."

"I'm sorry, sir. We have no one at Hungerford by that name. Perhaps you'd like to see one of our account executives?"

"Thank you."

She pressed a small button on the desk and a low chime sounded in some distant room. Almost immediately a replica of the receptionist appeared and walked briskly to the side of the desk.

"Would you take this gentleman to Mr. Attkins, please?"

The replica smiled a duplicate smile at Lyon. "This way, please."

The door from the reception area, activated by an electric eye, opened before them, and they entered a long hall lit by recessed spots built into the ceiling. Modern art of a subdued nature lined the hallway. With swishing skirt over cheerleader bottom and legs, she led the way past doors marked with such headings as Closing Room III. Around a corner the right wall turned to plate glass.

Lyon stopped before the long glass window to look into a computer room. Whirling disks on the machines seemed to turn at varying degrees of speed, and some reversed themselves to go first one way, then another. A printout spilled from another machine in long rolls of perforated lists. Two men in white lab coats moved silently around the cool, dehumidified room.

"This way, sir," the voice said nearly in his ear.

The small plaque on the large desk stated that its occupant was John Attkins, senior vice-president. Attkins wore a beige, well-tailored three-piece suit and had manicured hands with a Harvard class ring. He shook hands, smiled a plastic smile, and motioned Lyon to a chair.

"If you'll state your problem briefly, Mr. Wentworth, I'll try and see how Hungerford can fit into your financial picture."

"I have a small company in Connecticut. Perhaps you've heard of it, Lunch Breaks Unlimited?"

"No, I don't believe so. Is it listed?"

"I own one hundred percent of the stock. It's a food-vending service. We prepare sandwiches and meals that can be sold in a vending machine and heated in microwave ovens. Our clients are factories, schools, and office buildings."

"Yes, I'm aware of that type of operation. What is your need?"

"I've landed a contract with a very large industrial account that will require expansion of my warehouse, food service, and delivery staff."

"You have your own money-counting operation?"

"Yes. I have six Brandt coin-counting machines. We have daily armored car pickups. We're very careful."

"How much money do you need for expansion?"

"A quarter of a million."

"That could be arranged, under the right circumstances. You have certified financial statements and copies of your industrial contracts with you?"

"Yes, at the hotel. I didn't want to bring them unless you expressed an interest."

"I think possibly our equity operation might be interested. What happens, Mr. Wentworth, is that, simply stated, we take an ownership position in a company."

"I'm used to running my own shop."

"We wouldn't have it otherwise. You've undoubtedly built a successful operation and will continue to do so. We'd take a stock participation at a good price. The only foot we'd have in your door would be a few accounting people on your staff, and of course control of the money-counting operation. You can understand the reasons for that. There's always the potential for slippage when you deal with uncounted loose coins and bills."

"That's understandable. What's the next step?"

"If you'll bring your statements and contracts by here tomorrow at ten?"

"That would be fine. I assume that's when I can deal personally with Mr. Norkov?"

"Who?"

"Sergei Norkov. His name was suggested to me in Connecticut."

"You must be mistaken. We have no one here by that name."

"Pity. I had some information for him."

"Mr. Wentworth, do you want to meet further or not?"

"Of course."

Croft MacKenzie threw back his head with rolls of rocking laughter. "I love it!" he roared. "I just love it!"

"Do you think they'll be interested?"

"In the spools or your company? The answer to both is yes. Do you have financial statements to show them?"

"I borrowed them from a friend of mine who really does own the company."

The office of the Florida Anti-Organized Crime Force was only eight blocks from the Hungerford Company, but it could have been on the other side of the world. Where thick carpeting covered Hungerford's floors, dirty marble led to small office cubicles in an old post office building. Directions were not provided by pert ex-swimmers from Coral Gables, but from a sour-smelling old man leaning on a mop near a bucket of dirty water.

Pat's letter of introduction was addressed to Croft MacKenzie, a bulky man one pound this side of obesity with a massive head covered in white hair and a roar and manner that Lyon knew were the veneer of the professional country boy, but that he would never take as a sign of naiveté.

"Why their interest in a vending company? I only picked it because I had access to financial data."

"A cash flow without receipts. The clink of happiness to those jokers."

"The Vegas skim. Take in $x$ dollars and report $x$ minus $y$ to Uncle Sam?"

"Nope. The beauty of this operation is that it's the reverse of the skim. They put money into business."

"And report and pay taxes on it?"

"It's a laundering operation. One of the biggest problems facing all the families right now is getting their money to work for them in a manner that they can legitimately use. They have millions in cash flow from drugs, loan sharking, and prostitution. With the dollar unstable in Europe, and the difficulty in getting the money back, cash export is not feasible. They have to clean the money so they can use it."

"A vending company handles nickles, dimes, and quarters in bulk. They can feed money into the company as cash receipts, and there's no way to tell where it came from."

"Presto and it's laundered. Of course, once they take an equity position in a company, it's not long until they control it."

"And Sergei Norkov is behind it all?"

"He put it together and makes all the major decisions, and there's

137

not a damn thing we can do about it. The problem is, they appear lily white, always pay their taxes, never any visible strong arm stuff, and they're flanked with a staff of legitimate executives."

"And well run?"

"A model of corporate efficiency. We've penetrated as high as middle management, but still can't hang anything on them."

"The money they feed in has to come from several sources."

"From the major families throughout the country."

"Somewhere along the line there has to be a true accounting in order to divide the legitimate profits."

"We've never been able to penetrate that far."

"As they feed cash in, they'd eventually have to know where it came from and in what amounts in order to make a distribution of profits at some later time."

"For all we know, Sergei keeps that in his head."

"Maybe in the beginning, but it's gone on too long and is too large. It has to be recorded somewhere. Did Sergeant Pasquale tell you we're looking for something called the spools?"

"They could be anything."

"No, I don't think so. I know exactly what they are."

"Do you intend to tell the state of Florida, or am I supposed to ask if they're bigger than a bread box?"

"Reels of magnetic computer tape."

"Smoldering Jesus! Of course. The Hungerford Corporation has some of the finest computer hardware in town. With their present size the information would have to be recorded on magnetic tape."

"Known to only a few people. Nick Pasic, one of their oldest employees, would know where the reels were and what they contained."

"Christ! With that information, if we had those reels, we could blow their whole damn operation sky-high."

"Exactly. All we have to do is find where on the eastern seaboard Nick Pasic hid them."

"You won't find anything here," Croft said as he parked the car in the Pasic driveway. "We went over it with the proverbial fine toothed and someone else had been here before us."

Lyon and Bea stepped from the car into the bright Florida sunlight.

The house was similar to others on the street: slab base with cement block construction covered with stucco. There were jalousies and two orange trees in the front yard. A year-old Pontiac was parked under the carport, and in the backyard was a small camper.

"We did everything but use hammers on the concrete," Croft said. "There are no computer reels here."

"I wouldn't think there would be, but we may learn something." He took Bea's hand and walked around the rear of the house. She stopped at a garden that ran along the rear wall near the patio and stooped next to the flowers. "They're beautiful."

"Yes." Lyon looked over the small backyard and noted that the grass needed cutting. He turned to Croft. "Buried?"

"We ran over every square inch of yard with metal detectors. Net take: one dog chain, some coins, and a rusty penknife."

The interior of the house had been torn apart. Seat cushions and mattresses had been slit and ripped open, furniture was overturned, drawers pulled out, and fire hooks had been used to pull large hunks of plaster from the ceiling and walls.

Bea instinctively put her hand to her mouth as Lyon shook his head. "I gather neatness doesn't count."

"It's hard to search for something when you don't know what it is."

"What seems to be missing?"

"We have no way of knowing if there was any cash, jewelry, or other valuables here, but outside of that, we think some men's clothing is gone."

"What he took with him?"

"Probably."

Later, as Croft relocked the house, Bea entered the camper sweltering under the high sun. It too had been searched thoroughly and left in the same condition as the house. She stooped before an open drawer at the far end of the camper underneath the bunk. She called to Lyon. "What are these?"

Lyon entered the camper and knelt by her side. Before him, in jumbled heaps inside the drawer, were odd-shaped pieces of metal of various sizes. At the rear of the drawer were neatly bound lengths of nylon rope. He examined the pieces closely. "Do you see any pulleys?"

She rummaged through the stack of metal before holding up two pulleys. "Too small for clothesline."

"Not for nylon rope." He picked up a few of the pieces. "These are jam nuts; the pointed ones are pitons. This is a braking bar."

"GREAT, WENTWORTH. Next time I want a jam nut or piton, I'll know where to come. What are they?"

He held up a ring piton and ran an end of nylon rope through the ring. "The piton is driven into a rock crevice, the line goes through the ring, then you can use it to rappel, as a safety line, what have you."

"Rock climbing?"

"Yes. Good equipment and well maintained. Mr. Pasic was evidently an avid rock climber. Interesting."

They inspected the outside of the camper more closely. The rear windows and bumper were covered with stickers such as: I CLIMBED STONE MOUNTAIN, KENTUCKY—LAND OF THE BLUE GRASS, GREAT SMOKY MOUNTAINS NATIONAL PARK.

"It looks like he might have climbed every mountain in the Appalachian chain."

"Maybe," Lyon said.

They sat in the coolness of the smaller bar at their hotel. Croft had an ice-glazed glass of beer in front of him, Lyon his sherry, and Bea drank a tall frothy mixture of unknown ingredients. Croft took a long swig of beer and wiped foam from his mouth with the back of his hand.

"Okay, the spools are computer tapes and Pasic was a mountain climber."

"Rock climber. There's a little difference."

"And the killer wants you to find the spools so he can take them?"

"And sell them back to Hungerford."

"They aren't here, they aren't in Hartford, where are they?"

"Somewhere in between."

"Outside of climbing every rock for fifteen hundred miles, what now?"

"Pasic took a gamble, and he was certainly aware of the odds that he might be caught. He was evidently strong enough not to talk under physical torture, but was too careful a man not to have left a clue, a hint of where those reels are."

Bea took a sip of her drink. "Why did he do it in the first place? Why take the reels after nineteen years of service?"

"I don't think we'll ever know the full reason, but I don't think it was for money. I believe he intended to get back to his homeland where he felt he could hide, write a letter to either the FBI or Croft telling where the reels were hidden, and then disappear forever. He had enough money for his wants, had taken care of his daughter, and his wife was dead. His reasons probably had to do with what transpired between him and his wife as she died. It transformed him in some manner, changed his values."

From where Lyon sat in the cocktail lounge, he could see through the open door into the lobby and the reservation desk in the far corner. A man in a brightly flowered sports shirt and plaid slacks was bent over the counter filling out a registration form. There was something about the build and the back of his head . . . Lyon walked briskly into the lobby toward the desk.

"On vacation, Mr. Hilly?"

Hilly turned and stared at him. He took a step backward with his hands held protectively in front of him.

"Hey, no hard feelings, huh, Wentworth? I was in a jam and had to point that gun at you."

"I thought you were on bail."

"Hearing's three weeks from yesterday. A guy needs a vacation, right?"

**13** They stood in Hilly's hotel room in an awkward circle as the bellboy deposited a suitcase on the luggage rack and bustled around the room switching on air conditioning and lights. Hilly fumbled for a bill and tipped the bellboy.

"I don't remember calling this meeting," he said as the bellboy left.

"Call it an extemporaneous gathering," Croft said and jabbed a finger in Hilly's chest. The other man sat heavily down in a chair by the window. Lyon and Bea sat together on a far bed as Croft stood over Hilly. "The long arm of coincidence we don't buy."

"It's a big hotel, one of the best on the beach. Why can't I be here?"

"Are you clean?"

"They yanked my license and gun."

"If you're on bail, what are you doing down here?"

"My lawyer checked it out. As long as I'm back for the hearing, I'm all right."

"Where's your wife?" Bea asked softly.

"Home where she should be," was the snapped reply.

"You expect us to believe you're on vacation, and just happened to pick the same hotel where we are staying?"

"Believe what you want. Now, beat it! I want to take a shower."

He started across the room until Croft intercepted him and pushed him back in the chair. "Hey!"

"Shut up! Any more lack of cooperation from you and I'll see that you're booked."

"On what charge?"

"I can probably think of half a dozen to keep you occupied."

"I haven't done anything."

"You're here."

"I was told to be. I'm on a job."

"With a suspended license?"

Hilly shrugged. "A guy's got to make a living. I got a family to support."

"Who's your client this time?"

"An outfit called the Hungerford Corporation. A man named Attkins called me and said they had a security problem. They wired me a retainer and made my reservations here. Hell, I didn't know the Wentworths were going to be in Florida."

"A coincidence," Lyon said. "Like you just happened to be on your way to Connecticut when the bus was destroyed, and just happened to be watching me for some unknown client."

"I think I was suckered."

"What sort of security problem does Hungerford have?"

"I don't know. They said they'd explain when I got here."

"It seems to me that you're always in the wrong places at the right times."

"You know as well as I do that there's no evidence linking me to the murders. So, they got some charges against me. A fine and a year suspended is all I get when I cop a plea."

"You may be right," Lyon said.

Lyon appraised his wife as they waited for the elevator. She wore a sleeveless jade green sheath with matching teardrop earrings. "I like that outfit. Is it new?"

"Five years ago, Wentworth. Thanks for noticing."

In the hotel dining room they waited by the maître d's podium until a dark complexioned man in a tuxedo, carrying oversized menus, scurried toward them.

"A reservation for Wentworth."

The man's reaction was so immediate and marked that Lyon glanced at Bea to see if she'd palmed him a gratuity. "Of course, Mr. and Mrs. Wentworth. We are so happy to have you with us. Please come this way, Mr. Attkins is expecting you."

It was Bea's turn to glance at Lyon as they were led toward a secluded table in a far corner. As they approached, John Attkins stood and extended his hand toward Bea. "So good to meet you, Mrs. Wentworth."

A waiter hovered nearby until he received their cocktail order. "I didn't realize we had a dinner date, Mr. Attkins."

"As a senior officer of the company, I feel I have a responsibility during your stay in Miami. We offer a complete package of services to our clients."

"Including bribing the maître d' to call you about our dinner reservation."

Attkins smiled. "We steer a great deal of business here, which makes them most cooperative. We do seem to have run into one snag, Mr. Wentworth. It's about your company . . . Lunch Breaks Unlimited you called it."

"That's right."

"Information has come our way that the stock in that company is in fact held by a Mr. Heyman Shaw."

"I could be an intermediary for Mr. Shaw."

"Of course, but it is always so much easier if we all lay our cards on the table in the very beginning. I'm quite surprised to see you here, Mrs. Wentworth. We understand that you are running for Congress. You must be unopposed."

"I wish I were."

"I hope Mr. Croft MacKenzie was of help to you, Mr. . . . may I call you Lyon?"

"I assume you mean by that that Croft is what you call cooperative?"

"Many of the authorities in the area realize the worth of the Hungerford operation to the financial stability of Florida."

"That's reassuring."

"It must indicate to you the depth of our facilities."

"It certainly does. I assume you knew Nick Pasic?"

"He was one of our senior accountants. A loyal employee for nearly twenty years until something snapped. We conjecture that it's tied up with the tragic death of his wife last year."

"And what he took with him when he left."

"Nick had access to a great many important items in our company files. Information that would be of great worth to the competition. I think I can assure you that the recovery of such items would be of great benefit to us, and we would be prepared to pay you—shall we call it an honorarium?—for their return."

"What makes you think I can find them?"

Attkins smiled. "We don't like to leave any possibility uncovered at Hungerford. We have many avenues of approach to a problem. However, there are certain aspects of your background that intrigue me."

"I write children's books."

"Rather successfully, I'm told. But I have also heard that you are often involved in other matters."

"If I were to find the reels, what makes you think that I would turn them over to you?"

"Why not? We are a perfectly respectable business. We lend money and buy into companies. We are the heart's blood of capitalism: venture money."

"Someone else has already been trying to find the reels. At a cost of a lot of lives."

Attkins arched his eyebrow. "Someone else? Really, Mr. Wentworth." He opened the oversized menu with its old English lettering and turned to Bea. "The duck à l'orange is excellent here."

"I thought I'd try the scampi," she replied with a disarming smile.

"Does it worry you that eighteen people have died in the attempts to kill Pasic and get the reels?"

John Attkins looked up from the menu. His voice was low and modulated. "I do not worry about earthquakes in Greece either. The snails in garlic sauce are an excellent appetizer."

"I feel like melon."

"And you, Mr. Wentworth?" The ingratiating smile was becoming twisted. "Might I suggest . . . ?"

"My appetite has deserted me."

Attkins folded his menu, gathered the others, and placed them in a neat pile at the side of the table. They were immediately whisked away by the captain and fresh drinks served. "I was always taught that thoughtful men could speak reasonably and arrive at mutually satisfactory answers."

"That requires agreement on basic assumptions. I do not believe we're here to discuss dialectics, just as we are not prepared for a gourmet selection bought by the Hungerford Corporation."

"The company provides needed financial services. No one questions our morality when they play a juke box, buy a pack of gum from a vending machine, or stay in certain hotels we finance. Are the sins of our fathers carried to the sons?"

"I would prefer to discuss my business with Sergei Norkov in person."

"My father is quite ill with congestive heart failure and does not take an active part in the business anymore."

"It's a long way from the Lower East Side to Harvard, isn't it, Mr. Attkins?"

"And my father is quite concerned that the trend is not reversed."

"Laundering dirty money and arranging murder does not seem to be much in the way of upward mobility," Bea said.

John Attkins drank his drink and signaled for another with a flick of his finger. He seemed to anger, quickly brought it under control, and forced the smile back. "Your attitude is unctuous. Your morality, both of you, is a thin veneer that I could easily rip away." He turned almost vehemently toward Bea. "You! A politician for ten years. Can you say that you never made a deal? Never compromised a position to achieve your own end? Never played both ends of the fence for political reasons? Don't tell me you haven't."

Bea flushed. "You sound like my opponent. Yes, I've done the things you say. I work within a system that doesn't always work, that is built on compromise and the struggle between vested interests. But there is a difference. I have never knowingly compromised a position for another with the knowledge that the other side was backed by sources such as yours. Do you understand the difference?"

"Attkins has been laundered, like his money."

Attkins's eyes never left Bea's. "Your husband kills men."

"He had to."

"If we have finished establishing the parameters of our sanctimoniousness, I'd like to dispense with the hypocrisy. You see, Mrs. Wentworth, I know who your husband is and what he does."

"I write books."

"An interesting avocation, and probably the most unusual cover I've yet discovered. For quite some time now, my associates and I have been most curious about your identity. Mail drops and deposits of your payments in Swiss banks does not offer the protection in depth we usually require. However, your methods were always excellent, and we continued to utilize your services. It did annoy us last year when our agent, who was observing your mailbox in Tarrytown, was found floating in the Hudson River. Annoying, but we understood and respected your need for secrecy."

"Your voice is familiar. You're the one who has been calling me."

"Please don't continue the charade any further. It was quite obvious to me when I saw the newsreels of the bus passengers after the hijacking. Really, after that you could hardly expect to remain unknown to us."

"It wasn't my gun."

"Old habits are hard to break, aren't they? A bus that carried Nick Pasic—and our children's writer who just happened to be carrying a piece. Afraid of street crime, Mr. Wentworth?"

"Are you telling me that you don't know the identity of the man you hired to kill Pasic?"

"I do now. And I assume you have come in person to collect your fee—for Pasic and the return of the reels."

"I don't have them."

"Why did you hire Hilly?" Bea asked.

"He was rather close to the situation and might have information useful to me. As you know, I believe in covering all aspects of a problem. My associates are interviewing Mr. Hilly right now. I am sure he will cooperate. By the way, this is the last time we shall have such a discussion. In the future, I cannot take the chance that you might be wired. I will expect the reels to be delivered to my office in the morning. On the following day your money will be deposited to the usual account. Satisfactory?"

"And if I don't have the reels?"

"Then I would say you are in trouble."

147

"I need time. A week."

"Four days."

"FOR A MAN WITH ONLY THREE DAYS LEFT BEFORE THE COMBINED FORCES OF THE MAFIA AND ALL OF ORGANIZED CRIME COME AFTER HIM—YOU SURE KNOW HOW TO BLOW A DAY!"

Lyon opened one eye and half turned on the chaise longue set on the small balcony outside their hotel room. "Got my sherry? And where's your hearing aid?"

"Last time I swam with one on I brought in three CB channels." She handed him a pony of sherry, plucked the small device from the bedside table, and arranged it in her ear. "Okay, do we await our fate or what?" She adjusted the hem of her swimsuit.

"Why do women always do that?"

"Do what?"

"Adjust the bottom of their bathing suits like that?"

"Are you admiring, wondering, or merely being rhetorical?"

"All three. I have what I consider a marvelous suggestion."

"You should have thought of that earlier, Wentworth. Rocco's going to call, and look who's coming across the parking lot."

They both looked at the couple crossing the lot toward them. Raven had two cameras slung across his shoulders, and carried a small picnic basket in one hand while the fingers of the other intertwined with Kim's. There was a bouncy self-absorption about the couple as they moved toward the hotel.

Bea stood at the balcony rail and waved. "Hello, down there!"

Startled, Kim and Raven looked up and then waved back. In a two-handed basketball throw Raven catapulted the picnic basket toward the balcony. Lyon was forced to roll from his comfortable position on the recliner in order to grab the basket before it smashed into a glass-topped table.

Raven made a low bow toward Kim, laced his fingers together for her to step in, and hoisted her toward the balcony. He followed her by vaulting the rail and retrieving the wicker basket from Lyon. Within moments he had set up a miniature bar, signaled to Kim to get ice from the bucket in the bedroom, and began preparing drinks.

"I hope you can find the essence of a cherry for Bea's manhattan," Lyon said.

"But of course."

"I'll settle for an ordinary nontranscendental sherry."

"There will always be philistines amongst us." He continued his elaborate barkeeping ritual.

Bea shook her head. "Obviously you two had a good time, but did you find out anything?"

"Negative all the way. We checked out bus terminals in Washington, Richmond, Raleigh, Columbia, Atlanta, and a couple of smaller ones along the way. No one recognized the picture of Pasic."

"He was unobtrusive-looking. He could have slipped by."

Lyon nodded. "All right. That's all we can do in that area."

The phone rang and Bea answered. "Hi, Big Chief. What blows in the political winds up there? ... I see. I'm basking in the sun." She glanced at Kim. "They're saying I'm so unconcerned about the race that I came to Florida for a tan.... How do I stand on what? ... Abortion and gay rights? ... I know. It's not your fault. Here's Lyon."

Lyon took the phone and balanced a yellow legal pad on his knees. "What do you have?" He began to write notes. After five minutes he hung up and spread a road map across the bed next to some national geodetic maps he had purchased the day before. The others crowded around the bed as he began to draw a wiggly line from Miami to New York City.

"What information did Rocco have?"

"Credit slips from the American Express card in Collins's name." He traced the route on the map. "Collins, AKA Nick Pasic, picked up a rental car in Orlando, then drove to Pensacola, Florida. From there he went up into Alabama and over to Georgia at Columbus."

"How do you know all that?"

"He rented the car in Orlando. Gassed up at Pensacola and got gas again at Phoenix City, Alabama. That's just across the river from Columbus, Georgia. He stayed overnight in a motel outside of Atlanta. After Atlanta he gassed up again in Murphy, North Carolina, crossed into Tennessee, up to Nashville, then into Hopkinsville, Kentucky. He stayed overnight again at Willows, Kentucky."

Raven said, "He must have had a few while he drove. That's a crazy way to get to New York."

"From Kentucky into Ohio, a stop outside of Columbus, another slip from the Pennsylvania Turnpike, and then to New York, where he turned the car in."

Bea ran her finger along the line Lyon had traced on the map. "The route he took is at least 300 miles out of the way."

"He was trying to avoid detection."

"And to hide the reels somewhere along the route."

"You know, Lyon," Bea said, "we could spend the rest of our lives tracing that route and trying to find those things." She looked pensive a moment. "What about dates? Did he spend more time in one place than another?"

Lyon glanced down at the pad. "We don't know where he was between Miami and Orlando, but we do know about those stops in Atlanta, Murphy, and Willows, Kentucky."

"That's not much help. What else did Rocco say?"

"That the credit card in the name of Collins was based on a false ID that Pasic had been building for nearly a year, and it even extended to his obtaining a passport in that name."

"I can use that," Raven said. "How did he arrange it?"

"It's time-consuming but not difficult. Any library has back newspapers. You pick a year, usually the same as your own date of birth, and pick out lists of birth announcements. You keep checking names until you find one that died as an infant. You apply for a birth certificate, by mail, in that name, Social Security card, driver's license, and passport. Pasic even established bank accounts and obtained credit cards in the name of Collins."

"Then he's planned this since his wife died?"

"It would seem so."

"Then the computer reels aren't stuck away in any old place. A great deal of thought went into where he secreted them."

"Rocco also said that some characters from Rhode Island have been in town asking about us."

"One of the families?"

"That explains how Attkins had so much information on us."

"What do you think about Attkins's remark about Croft's 'cooperation'?"

150

Lyon shrugged. "I don't know. But we can't take any chances. The innuendoes have destroyed our ability to use Croft."

Bea began to align copies of the geodetic maps alongside the road map with mounting excitement. "We found mountain-climbing things in the Pasic camper. Just suppose he were going to hide those things in a place almost inaccessible to the ordinary person. A high place, rock cliffs, where only the most experienced climber could go." She ran her fingers along the maps. "Look, outside of Bryson City, North Carolina, there's a place called Nantahala Gorge. See how the contour lines merge together above the road? That means a nearly sheer cliff rises straight up from the valley."

Kim nodded agreement and pulled another projection across the bed. "Right, hon. But look at Willows, Kentucky. I've been through there and the place is filled with limestone cliffs."

"What did you say?" Lyon asked.

"Willows is a dinky little place in the middle of the mountains and miles away from anything."

"You said limestone cliffs?"

"Yes, you know, those little skeletons that piled on top of each other millions of years ago and are now mountains."

"There's Kennesaw Mountain outside of Atlanta," Raven said. "And he did spend time near Atlanta."

Bea slapped the maps in dejection. "It's impossible! Most of his nutty trip north was either in or near mountains. Even if we knew which specific mountain and which particular cliff . . . it would still be impossible to find the reels."

Lyon stretched out on the vacant twin bed and crossed his arms behind his head. "Pasic spent too much time and took too much risk on the theft of the computer reels . . . he was a meticulous and methodical man. He would have left us word where he hid them."

"I think it died with him."

"No," Lyon said slowly. "I don't think it did. In fact, I think he left a map telling us exactly where to look."

# 14

"WENTWORTH, WHAT IN HELL ARE YOU TALKING ABOUT!"

"You had better adjust your hear . . ."

"I CAN HEAR. I'M MAD! If you know the answers, tell us."

"In due time, hon." Lyon began to fold the maps neatly.

Bea turned toward Raven and Kim. "He's that way, you know. What are we going to do? I'll tell you what we're going to do. We're going to go along with him."

"I'd like to know where we're going," Raven said with his usual smile.

"Different places. Bea and I will go to Atlanta to pick up something, and Raven, if you'll drop Kim off in Orlando?"

"You want a trace on what Nick Pasic was doing there, how long he stayed, where, and so forth?"

"Right, if Raven doesn't mind helping?"

"Hell, no. This is great material. I wouldn't miss it for the world."

"Okay, after you drop Kim off, meet us at the Holiday Inn in Bryson City, North Carolina."

"Then you do think the reels are in Nantahala Gorge?"

"Our first problem is to get out of the hotel undetected. It's still possible that Hilly is watching us. I'm sure Attkins has others keeping us under scrutiny, and Croft MacKenzie and his men are also lurking around."

"We could hold a convention."

"Their sheer numbers will help us. I want Raven and Kim to leave the hotel by way of the balcony, climb down to the parking lot, and take the car Bea and I rented to Orlando."

"They'll see it's not you before we're halfway there," Raven said.

"Probably, but in the meantime we'll have time to get out a different way."

"Sounds good," Kim said. "Raven and I go over the balcony dressed in your clothes and take your car."

"Exactly."

"Just one thing," the black woman said. "If we're going to do this, might I suggest that we do it at night? Otherwise, I have the feeling it's not going to work."

Once they reached the outskirts of the city, Lyon stopped and made a phone call to Connecticut.

"You want it on the plane tonight," Rocco grumpily acknowledged.

"Or first thing in the morning so that it arrives in Atlanta early."

"I'll have to go through Pat."

"Whatever you have to do, Rocco. It's important."

It was daylight when they arrived in Atlanta and checked into a motel. They left a wake-up call for ten, and both fell onto the bed fully clothed and slept.

The phone awoke Bea. She thanked the operator for the call and shook Lyon.

He groaned and turned over. "Wake me in an hour."

"We've got things to do."

He sat up. "Right. I have some shopping to do before I get to the airport."

"And I make phone calls," she said as Lyon went into the bathroom to throw water on his face. "You think I should try the local colleges first?"

"I think that would be the best bet. I'll be back in two hours."

As they drove toward northern Georgia, the red clay of the lowlands turned to the rolling hills heralding the beginning of the Appalachian Mountains. Bea drove, weaving past tractors on the shoulder of the road, while Lyon sat next to her, holding tightly to the package Rocco had sent air express.

She glanced at the package. "And that's the map in there?"

"I hope so."

"And the stuff in the back seat?"

"A pack, canteen, nylon ropes, ice ax, pitons, flashlights."

"We're going climbing?"

"In a manner of speaking."

"When was the last time you climbed rocks?"

"I had a course in the army once."

"That was a long time ago."

"Then there was the time my balloon went down on Talcott mountain."

"The rescue squad brought you down."

"Well, my ankle was broken."

"I hope this guy I called at the college is the man you want."

"An assistant professor at North Georgia College in Dahlonaga, and he has the other qualifications?"

"So he claims."


Assistant Professor of Geology Kai Nordstrom was a vague man. His small office was located in one of the older buildings on the campus. A large window ran the full length of the rock-cluttered room near a rolltop desk whose surface was covered with more rocks of all sizes and shapes and a pile of uncorrected student themes. He leaned back in the ancient swivel chair with his hands clasped behind his head and smiled at them.

"You're the Worthingtons, right? Tiger Worthington, funny name. I expected to see you drive up on a motorcycle or at least a skateboard. Suppose you're interested in North Georgia rocks. We have diamonds up here, did you know that? I can show you where to look, if you're interested. Or do you want to pan for gold? No money in it, but it's fun. Give me your map and I'll show you where to go, Mr. Worthington."

Lyon shook the professor's hand. "Wentworth. Lyon Wentworth."

"Well, I was fairly close." He looked out the window and put his feet on the desk. "They shouldn't let girls wear such short-short shorts on campus. Disconcerting, very disconcerting. They tell me that if I got married, I wouldn't notice such things. What kind of rocks are you looking for?"

Bea had a strong sense of dèjá vu, and the feeling that perhaps her husband was not as unique as she had thought. She looked from Lyon to Nordstrom, and found that although the teacher was a few years younger, they were very similar in appearance. My God, the man didn't wear socks either.

"We're not looking for rocks," Lyon said. "But I wonder, if you looked at this, could you tell me what it's a map of?" He unwrapped the package he had picked up earlier at the airport and handed Nordstrom the copy of *The Wobblies' Revenge* that he and Nick Pasic had inscribed for Mark.

The geologist looked at the book, puzzled, until Lyon opened it to the flypiece and the odd drawing below Pasic's inscription to his grandson:

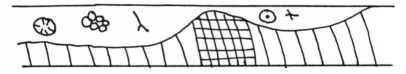

"Uh huh," the geologist mumbled.

"You are an officer of the National Speleological Society?"

"Yes, I am." He examined the drawing again.

"If I mentioned the name Willows, Kentucky, would that help?"

"Oh, sure. The Willows. I've been in it."

"Can you read the map for me?"

"You mean, tell you what the symbols mean?"

"Yes."

"Sure." He spread the book on the desk and his whole manner seemed to change. The distant quality that had struck Bea so forcibly when they entered disappeared as he bent over the carefully drawn cave map. He found a pair of dividers under the uncorrected papers, and calibrated various portions of the drawing. Standing, he went to a file drawer in the corner and pulled a larger drawing from the bottom drawer and spread it across the floor. He looked first at the larger drawing and then back to Pasic's smaller rendition.

"The small drawing in the book is a partial cave map, and my guess is that it's a passage in the Willows Cave. The approach is through an internal shaft from the main passage. That's this symbol." He indicated the configuration ⊛ .

"This particular tunnel has a stream and siphon in it. This grouping here ⊛ indicates a rock fall. There are stalagmites, and on the other side of the siphon is a pillar on a ledge. This $x$ mark near the pillar could mean anything."

"You say an internal shaft. How deep is it?"

The professor examined the larger cave map. "Thirty feet, according to my elevations. Not a bad climb."

"And the siphon, that means the stream goes under rock, but the passage enlarges on the other side? Can we get through that siphon?"

"Oh, sure. It's only about ten feet, and there's a ledge on the other side."

"Could that $x$ next to the pillar beyond the siphon mean someone hid something there?"

"It could mean anything whoever drew this map wanted it to mean."

"Can I get to that spot?"

"Sure, if you were an experienced caver."

"Could a neophyte make it?"

"I suppose, although a siphon is a scary thing for someone not used to them. You have to understand that the Willows is not a show cave."

"Show cave?"

"One that's generally open to the public. Show caves like Monmouth, Carlsbad Caverns, and so forth, have tour guides, interior lighting, and paths. The Willows has only one known entrance, and that's on private property. It's not really a spectacular cave when you consider others in the area."

"Then not many would enter it in a given year?"

"A dozen maybe. Fewer yet would go past the siphon. There's no real reason to go in the area marked on your map. As you can see, the stream widens out again, but then the passage stops. It's a dead end that would be of no real interest to a caver."

"Would Pasic put the computer reels in a cave?" Bea asked.

"What better place than a location with a constant cool temperature? Mr. Nordstrom, could you give us directions as to how to find the location of that shaft?"

"I wouldn't recommend it."

The man in the black Chevrolet, far down the road past the campus gates, yawned and lowered his high-powered binoculars. The glasses gave him a clear view of the Wentworths standing near a large window in the geology building. He imagined they'd leave soon in their car to wherever they were going.

The device he had attached under their car would allow him to stay back. Within a few-mile radius, the signal device would alert him if they veered from the road or changed direction. He yawned again. It would be a simple tail. He checked the road on either side. His eyes swept past a small boy on a big wheel toy and discounted any danger. He was careful, always careful, and that had allowed him to survive.

"Why do you want to go into the Willows, son?" The old man rocked slowly on the porch. His face was grizzled and the overalls were spotted, but his eyes were clear and inquiring.

Lyon stood before the porch with one foot on the bottom step. "We're looking for something, Mr. Bartram."

"My brother died in the Willows. Did that professor tell you that?"

"No, sir. He didn't."

"Yep. Back in '08. He was playing in there, and he ran back from the entrance and fell down one of them holes and broke his neck. My Pap put rocks in the entrance, and for twenty years no one went in the Willows."

"It's very important to us, Mr. Bartram."

"It's your neck. The professor tell you the price?"

"I brought it with me." He handed a paper bag to the outstretched hands of the old man. The thin fingers lifted the bottle of bourbon by the neck. He squinted at the label.

"This bond?"

"Best there is."

"All right. Here's the key."

"A key to a cave?" Bea asked.

157

"Ten years ago I put a fence across the entrance. Didn't want no kids going in there. I keep it locked. You take the key and bring it back to me when you come out. If you don't bring it back, and I got to go up there and lock the gate again, no one else goes in the Willows —forever. Now, when you people be back?"

"Not later than six."

"Hold you to that. If you aren't out by six, I go to Ledley's place down the road and call the sheriff to come find your bodies."

"That's reassuring," Bea said.

"Mr. Bartram, if the gate is locked, you would have had to give the key to anyone else going into the Willows."

"Only way in we know of."

"In the past two weeks or even the past month, has anyone else gone in?"

"Nope. A group went in last summer. They were the last."

Lyon turned from the porch in disappointment. "Are we still going in?" Bea asked.

"May as well since we're here. I don't see how I could have been wrong." He shouldered the pack. They waved to the old man on the porch and began the long walk up the hill toward the cave entrance, which was shrouded in brush and trees at the top.

"Six, or we come after the bodies," the old man yelled after them.

Their breath came in short gasps at the unaccustomed exertion of climbing the steep embankment. Scrub pine and heavy brush dotted the landscape, although there was a stand of willow trees flanking the cave entrance. As they neared the top, they saw the heavy wire mesh stretched across the narrow cave opening. Long spikes had been sledged into the limestone cliff and secured the fence on either side of the opening. A wooden door frame with a sturdy gate had been built into the mesh.

Lyon let the pack slip from his shoulders and ran ahead. He stood by the gate and examined the lock before turning toward Bea who trudged up the last of the hill.

"The lock's been jimmied. It's broken, Bea. Someone *has* been in here since last summer."

They stood before the open gate and looked in the entrance. Afternoon light from the west fell through the willows over their shoulders and lit the entryway for a dozen feet. Lyon dug two waterproof flashlights from the pack and handed one to Bea.

She switched on her light and strode into the cave. Her light bobbed up and down, casting patterns across the floor and walls as the passageway began a downward slope. The walls were bare and mostly smooth, while the flooring seemed to be composed of a mixture of sand and dirt.

She stopped and turned off her light. The blackness was complete. The passageway, in addition to its downward incline, had also veered away from the entrance.

Where was Lyon? She switched the light on and pointed it toward the rear. "Lyon!" Her shout died without echo. She called again, "Lyon!"

He rounded a distant bend carrying his head thrust forward between hunched shoulders. The flashlight, clenched tightly in one hand, shone directly at his feet. When he shuffled forward in his awkward gait, she could hear the rasp of his breathing, each intake of air making a sharp cutting sound. He passed her, his gaze intent on the passage floor immediately to his front, each step a measured mechanical placement of one foot before the other. She let her light pass across his face and saw that his eyes were wide, nearly glazed, and small beads of perspiration studded his forehead.

Bea knew that her husband was in the throes of deep terror. She ran after him and nearly tripped on the now uneven surface that was dotted with small rocks and boulders. Her hand touched his arm without response until she shook his shoulder.

"Lyon, what is the matter?"

He mopped his brow with a bandanna without taking his eyes from the floor. When he spoke, his voice was low. "I don't know how much further I can go."

"You're . . ." She could not use the word. "You look very uncomfortable."

He laughed with a hollow sound. "Understatement, my dear. Quite an understatement." The rasping breath continued.

"Sit down."

They sat with their backs against the wall. She found the canteen in his pack and drank, passed it to Lyon, and watched him take a long drink. He seemed to make a conscious effort to control his breathing until it gradually returned to normal.

159

"I didn't think it would be this bad."

"This is why you wanted me along on this trip?"

He nodded.

"We shouldn't have come."

"It has to be done."

"Someone else could have come in here. We could have called Rocco, Kim, and Raven, anyone else. I never knew you had this feeling."

"You ever hear me suggest a spelunking holiday?"

"You've always known?"

Lyon leaned against the rock and closed his eyes. "If I pretend, perhaps I can fantasize that I'm in my balloon."

"How did this happen?"

"I've never cared for close, narrow places, even as a child, but it became worse in Korea. It was toward the end and I went up to Rocco's forward position for a game of poker. We were in a bunker when a large shell landed. It burst near the entrance and collapsed the whole damn thing on us. We were in there two days before they got us out."

She jerked to her feet. "Okay, back we go." She reached for his hands. "No macho bit, let's just get out of here. I don't like flying and you don't like caving."

He turned toward the descending tunnel. "We have to get those reels."

"Let some trained spelunkers do it."

"It has to be us." He shuffled down the passage.

Bea stood looking at the retreating light then hurried to catch up.

Lyon stopped and shone his light on the large cave map Nordstrom had given him. The passage had narrowed considerably, and ahead he could see where the bedding plane lowered toward the floor creating a squeeze slightly more than a foot high. He checked the scale on the map and looked up toward the narrow opening. Bea caught up to him, looked at the squeeze and then at her husband.

"You think we'll fit?"

"Map says we do."

She slipped the knapsack from his shoulders, extracted a thin nylon line, and tied it to a pack strap. She hunched over in the passage to make her way into the squeeze and looped the line to her belt. She

160

lay on the floor and began to work her way awkwardly through the squeeze. It was difficult to grip the light and crawl, and now she knew why experienced cavers often wore miner's hats.

It was a long squeeze that lasted fifty yards, although the passage opened slightly to a height of nearly two feet. Her scrabbling movement slowly pushed her forward as sharp protuberances nicked her knees and elbows.

She paused for breath and shone the light ahead. The squeeze ended a few yards ahead and opened into a large cavern room. Bea exited from the narrow aperture and stood erect. She swiveled her light across the larger space.

The room was thirty to forty feet in width and nearly that in height. Flashing her light ahead, she could not make out the extent to which the cavern room extended. Pencil-thin stalactites hung in Christmas-tree-like rows from the ceiling, while stalagmites grew from the cavern floor and reached toward their dripping partners on the ceiling.

She found it breathtaking, and slowly walked along the side of the room studying a group of calcite crystals growing on the walls in myriad shapes and forms. They seemed to wink in her light and cast a blue shadowy glow along the walls.

The rasp behind her made her turn. Lyon had made it to the room and was huddled in the corner with the wavering light held in his shaking hand.

"This is ridiculous. We can't go on," she said.

His hand, trembling over the map, waved at her. "At the end of this room there is a phreatic tube on the right. We take that for nearly a quarter of a mile until we reach another room similar to this. There will be three shafts in that room. The third one is where Pasic's map begins."

"How far?"

"We'll be a mile in and eight hundred seventy-five feet down."

"I'll lead. Just tell me what a phreatic tube is, so when I come across one I'll know it."

He lay on the floor with his head pillowed on the knapsack and closed his eyes. "Limestone caves are formed by water seepage that erodes the rock. Phreatic passages are formed by water under exteme pressure that's subsequently changed course."

"For a claustrophobic you know a lot about caves."

"When I had the mumps overseas there wasn't anything to read but a book about . . ."

"I know. How are you feeling?"

"Better." He forced his body to relax by starting with the lower extremities and imagining their anatomical makeup. He willed the various nerves in the lower portion of his body to relax, and then his midsection and arms. He lay limp against the rock and thought of animals that lived in caves. Bats, salamanders, and worms. The book *The Cricket in the Cave* might work. Bird's nest soup in China was made from certain types of nests found only in Java caves: that was an interesting fact he might incorporate in the book. The Wobblies didn't fear caves, but then again, the Wobblies didn't fear much of anything.

He felt them near him.

They moved down the length of the room to flank the entrance of the phreatic tube. Their tails swished back and forth while red eyes peered through the deepest possible darkness.

Lyon Wentworth got to his feet and followed his wife and imaginary beings into a passageway he could not have otherwise entered.

They stopped at the yawning blackness of the shaft indicated on Nick Pasic's map. Bea shone her light into the depths. The opening was nearly a perfect circle with a diameter of fourteen feet. Lyon turned away from the shaft to take pitons and an ice ax from the pack. He felt along the wall for fissures, found a narrow slit, and pounded his piton. Looping a line through the ring, he tugged until completely satisfied that it was secure enough to support their weight.

"I don't suppose you've ever rappelled?"

"All the time. Whenever our garden club runs out of speakers, someone always suggests that we rappel down a cliff or two. Wentworth, you know how I hate heights."

He adjusted the rope around his body. "We make a great pair." He showed her how to place the rope, and then stood at the lip of the shaft, facing away from the opening, and leaned backward. Gripping the rope, he leaped off the edge and bounced off the side of the shaft halfway down. He bounced again and then reached the bottom. "Lower the pack next and then yourself."

For the first time the complete silence of the cave was broken.

162

Water gurgled nearby. As Lyon swiveled the flashlight he could see the small stream as it came through the rock, widened, and then disappeared under rock at the siphon.

He turned the light upward to see Bea, halfway down the shaft, with her feet braced against the rock. Her body swayed. "Let out more slack and jump off."

"ARE YOU CRAZY!"

"You stay like that much longer and your arms will tire and you'll be in real trouble."

"IF THIS ISN'T TROUBLE, I DON'T KNOW WHAT IS." She began to lower herself on the rope until he was able to reach up and pull her down to the floor. "ONE THING, WENTWORTH. How do we get back up?"

"Hand over hand."

As the map indicated, near the shaft was a pile of fallen rock, and then the stream widened to fill the passage as rock and water met to form a seemingly impenetrable passage. They walked as far as they could on the shelf and looked into the water. "The siphon."

"The professor said it was only a few feet until the roof became higher and there was another shelf." Bea heard his breathing become more rapid and knew that any delay would not help matters. She tied the end of a line to her waist, sat on the edge of the shelf with her feet in the water, and pushed off.

The cold water shocked her. She took a deep breath, and holding the waterproof flashlight before her, began an awkward swimming movement through the siphon. There was only blackness ahead, and she had a brief moment of panic. They were following a map found in a children's book, and were taking the word of a fey disoriented professor that the siphon ended in an air pocket. She took a stroke upward and felt her fingernails brush against rock. She knew she must have come more than a dozen feet, the supposed length of the passage. It could go on . . . and on . . . an underground stream whose current would carry her on forever.

Her hand broke from the surface, and then her head and shoulders. She gulped air as her free hand clawed for the ledge.

She placed the light on the shelf and pulled herself from the water. Untying the rope from her waist, she wrapped it around the pillar and began to wait for Lyon.

She knew he was a strong swimmer, and with the safety line attached, should have little difficulty; but still he did not come. She gave the line two hefty tugs and felt a tug in return.

Lyon's head surfaced. His eyes were wide and blinking as she reached for him with both hands and helped him to the ledge.

"The reels should be behind the pillar." He scrabbled around the pillar and knelt to scoop sand and loam with his hands. Within minutes he had uncovered a metal box encased in a plastic waterproof bag. He tore off the bag, opened the box, and turned the light on the two computer reels. "We've got them!" He turned to see Bea standing on the ledge beyond the pillar looking into the water.

"Maybe not for long." She pointed to a glow in the water coming from the siphon. "Someone's coming."

# 15

"Do you know who it is?"

Lyon looked at the wavering light refracted through the dark waters of the siphon. "Yes, I think I do. When he surfaces, he'll be disoriented for a few moments, which means we'll only have seconds."

"To do what?"

"To get into the water and go back the way we came."

They stood poised on the edge of the ledge with their lights switched off. The glow from the siphon grew stronger, an arm holding a flashlight broke the surface, and it was followed by the head and shoulders of a man. The beam traversed the narrow ledge illuminating Bea and Lyon. The swimmer's orientation quickly returned and he scrabbled toward the ledge and heaved himself from the water.

"Now!" Lyon yelled and dove for the siphon entrance. An instant backward glance before he submerged revealed Raven Marsh crouched on the ledge activating the slide of a large automatic. With strong strokes, Lyon swam for the bottom of the siphon in the hope that Bea had entered the water before him.

A zip close to his ear.

Raven had snapped off a shot.

He swam easily through the tunnel and wondered why the return passage was so much easier. He realized, with horror, that the rapidity of his movement was due to not carrying the flashlight. He had dropped it on the ledge as he dove into the water. If the siphon branched, if there were other tunnels that he mistakenly took . . . He kept swimming until he saw a glow to his front. Bea was swimming awkwardly, her flashlight still in her hand. He saw her stroke upward and followed.

They sat on a rock near the internal shaft, regaining their breath, until Lyon put his hand on his wife's shoulder. They scrambled to their feet and stumbled toward the ropes hanging down the shaft. She hesitated, her hands limply grasping the lines.

"We don't have much time. Hold the rope tight. Brace your feet and pull yourself up. That's right . . . keep your feet against the wall. Hurry!"

She started slowly up the shaft. He waited until she was nearly to the top before he followed.

They lay on the tunnel floor at the head of the shaft. "What now?"

"He'll be along in a moment." Lyon went to the lip of the shaft and pulled up the ropes.

"The reels!"

"I think we can be sure he'll bring them."

Over the soft sound of the stream at the bottom of the shaft, they heard the crunch of shoes on rock, and then a light flickered off the walls.

"Wentworth! You up there?" Raven Marsh's voice echoed from the bottom of the well. "Goddamn it! I know you're there. Answer me and we'll make a deal."

Lyon placed a finger over Bea's lips.

"Come on. Throw me a line!"

"A line for the reels," Lyon called without exposing himself.

"You're holding the deck. You've got a deal."

Lyon lay prone near the lip and coiled a line.

"Don't," Bea said. "You can't believe him."

"I know," he replied in a whisper and threw the line over the edge. He slithered toward a rock to brace himself. "The reels first, Raven. If I feel more than their weight, I let go."

"They're coming."

166

Lyon tugged on the line. As the weight began to ascend he estimated it to be the reels, or at least not a man on the end of the rope. The package came over the rim and Bea, without exposing herself, undid the line and opened the box. She nodded toward Lyon.

"Okay, Wentworth. I did my half. Send the line back."

"In a minute." He felt around the cave floor until he found a heavy rock he could hold in one hand. "You'll need both hands to catch this, Raven."

The man below wedged his light on a rock. "I'm ready."

"Here it comes." Lyon dropped the rock on the flashlight. The light shattered under the impact and winked out.

"Hey!"

"Come on, Bea. Let's get out of here." The glaze returned to Lyon's eyes as he stumbled along the tunnel. Bea walked behind him with the box of computer reels under one arm, while the other steadied the light beam on his path.

They still heard the decreasingly distinct screams from the man at the bottom of the shaft.

"Wentworth, you promised! Goddamn you! Where are you! Throw me a light!"

The shots began. They stopped to look back. The discharge of the heavy pistol caused a lightning effect in the tunnel, while the whine of the ricochets bouncing off walls and ceiling seemed like the cry of a hurt animal.

The tunnel swerved to the right, obliterating the sounds of gunfire.

They began to hurry up the incline toward the cave entrance. As they rounded the last turn of the tunnel, and saw the dim light of the entrance in the distance, Lyon began to run. He stumbled in the soft sand of the floor as he staggered out into daylight.

He sank to the ground with his back against a willow tree. His shirt was soaked in perspiration, his breathing erratic, and his pulse rate astronomical. Normalcy began to return as he looked across the green valley spread below the hill. In the distance, a large hawk circled in slow sweeping banks.

"We had better get help," Bea said.

"I would think so." He got to his feet and walked back to the cave entrance. "I think we better lock him in."

"You're not going back in there?"

"Lord, no! But he's not coming out either." He closed the gate across the entrance and extracted a piton from his belt and pounded it through the hasp. "I think that will hold him until we get help up here."

The living room furniture at Nutmeg Hill had been shifted into a corner and a large blackboard placed in front of the fireplace. The board was divided into squares for each precinct in the congressional district. Kim stood ready to insert the vote totals as they came over the bank of telephones installed along the far side of the room.

An aura of expectancy filled campaign workers as they milled nervously through the house and spilled out onto the patio.

The subdued babble of election night activity provided a muted background for Rocco and Lyon as they sat in the study with drinks in hand. Rocco swirled the ice in his glass and glanced at his watch. "It's nearly eight and the polls are closing. They ought to have the results soon."

"Bea's got a worker in every polling place in the district. As soon as the machines are opened the calls will begin to come in. We should know in a few minutes."

"Since the beginning of the campaign I've had the feeling that you didn't really want to go to Washington."

Lyon felt the aura of the familiar room where he had spent so many of his waking hours. It was an integral part of him, almost an extension of his self—a comfortable retreat and a place of work. He knew, without looking, the view from the window by the desk that extended past the patio and parapet and overlooked the winding Connecticut River below the bluff now splotched with streaks of silver light. "I'm part recluse and part creature of habit. I like things I'm used to, but Bea wants to go to Washington, and I know she can do some good down there. I can work anywhere, Washington as well as Murphysville. Well, I can work almost anywhere, as long as it's above ground."

Rocco pulled on the last of the vodka and poured a refill from the bar cart. "At least you made it back for the election. For a while, I was afraid you and Bea were going to become permanent residents of Kentucky."

"Actually, they were very sympathetic and did their best to speed up the hearings. Needless to say, it got a little complicated to explain."

"You know, I still think that Raven Marsh killed himself. Hell, if I'd been down in that black hole and thought I'd been left there permanently, I might have, too."

"In a sense he did, according to the coroner in Kentucky, but not purposely. He began firing as we left him, and one of the bullets ricocheted from the wall and caught him in the forehead. He probably died about the time Bea and I were making our way through that damnable squeeze. Thank God it's over."

"If it helps any, just before I came up here tonight we had a conference call with the Florida Task Force and the FBI. They've completed running the computer tapes and the printouts are very interesting. The IRS wants first crack at the Hungerford Corporation, and then there will be a grand jury hearing for further indictments. It's going to take a while, but the whole damn operation will be dismantled, and they foresee a couple dozen charges against members of the families throughout the country. Your telephone caller friend, Attkins, will be the first under the ax."

"Sergei Norkov?"

"He had a massive heart attack the minute he was told you had recovered the reels. He's in an intensive care unit at a Miami hospital. They doubt he'll make it through the week. They tell me he had a past history of heart trouble."

"I heard that from his son."

"You know, old buddy, there are a few pieces missing. Like, how were you so sure the reels were in a cave, specifically the Willows?"

"In looking back, I see now that I was Nick Pasic's insurance. That night in the hotel room, he did everything but write me a detailed confession. It couldn't have been more obvious now that I think of the inscription he wrote to his grandson in my book."

"Which was a cave map."

"It took me a while to realize that, but it fit when I remembered the line he wrote about the secret of the karst."

"That doesn't mean anything to me."

"Pasic was Yugoslavian by birth. The karst area of that country has given its name to all karst formations of limestone throughout the world."

"Which are usually filled with caves?"

"Exactly. And then there was another hint, the alias he used, F.

Collins. Floyd Collins, the name of the caver who died in Sand Cave in 1925."

"That rings the gong. Wasn't he the cave explorer who became trapped underground for days and died just before they were able to rescue him?"

"Uh huh."

"Then when Bea found the rock-climbing equipment in Pasic's camper, you discounted mountains and thought of caves."

"It's as hard to go down as up."

"And then when I came across the credit card charge that showed Pasic had been in Willows, Kentucky...."

"The reels had to be there. The cave map told us exactly where."

"I've got that part. How did you suspect Raven Marsh?"

"I couldn't be positive until I saw who it was that came after us in the cave. I knew it had to be someone that was close to the situation, someone we'd had contact with. I first began to suspect Raven when I asked him about his articles and the sale of North American serial rights. Although he purported to be a writer, he gave me an indirect answer."

"So you sent Kim to check out Orlando to get her out of the way and leave Raven open to follow you."

"Yes, and it worked, although I'm hazy on exactly how he traced us to the Willows."

"I can answer that one. When Kim reached Orlando, she began to worry about you and Bea going off alone. She called me, and during the conversation I told her about the package I sent air freight to Atlanta."

"That explains it. Raven picked me up at the Atlanta airport and followed us to the Willows."

"As far as the rest is concerned, I suppose that all Raven's contacts with Attkins were by mail and Swiss bank deposits?"

"Attkins never did believe that I wasn't his hit man, although he should have begun to wonder when he made me that bonus offer over the telephone and then a few days later got a letter demanding a hundred thousand for the spools."

"And no one else knew about the bonus offer until we heard the phone call recording in my office."

"When Hilly and Raven were present. Until that time Raven